SEE YOU AGAIN

KAIT NOLAN

For Dennie.
Because I won the Mother-in-Law Lottery

A LETTER TO READERS

Dear Reader,

This book is set in the Deep South. As such, it contains a great deal of colorful, colloquial, and occasionally grammatically incorrect language. This is a deliberate choice on my part as an author to most accurately represent the region where I have lived my entire life. This book also contains swearing and sex between the lead couple, as those things are part of the realistic lives of characters of this generation, and of many of my readers.

If any of these things are not your cup of

tea, please consider that you may not be the right audience for this book. There are scores of other books out there that are written with you in mind. In fact, I've got a list of some of my favorite authors who write on the sweeter side on my website at https://kaitnolan.com/on-the-sweeter-side/

If you choose to stick with me, I hope you enjoy!

Happy reading!

Kait

CHAPTER 1

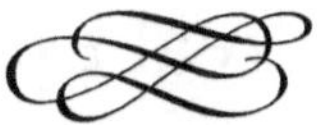

"THIS IS ALL YOUR fault." Trey Peyton glared at the owner of the big brown eyes, who couldn't seem to care less about the wreck she'd just caused.

She just blinked at him, all innocence, as if she wasn't the reason his sensible sedan was currently nose-first in a ditch. Given how fast he'd been going when he came over that hill, he was lucky he *only* had a flat.

Sucking in a breath, he scooped a hand through his hair and searched for some calm. "Oh, excuse me. Where are my manners? Let me introduce myself. I'm Gerald Peyton, III, CEO of Peyton Consolidated."

She ignored the hand he offered.

"Never heard of it? It's a multi-billion-dollar corporation. Mostly real estate and hotels these days. Though I've been dipping my toes into urban redevelopment and rural tourism lately. Maybe you've seen some of the stuff my company has done in Wishful? The Babylon is a top-rated boutique hotel and spa. Or maybe you've been to The Madrigal Theater since it was restored?"

His audience twitched one hip, restless.

"Am I boring you? My apologies. You know, that notion that billionaires only drive pretentious sports cars that cost as much as a normal person's house is really a stereotype. Although maybe if I'd been truer to form, I'd have actually managed to stay *on* the road when I swerved to avoid your sizable ass."

Unconcerned with the insult, the cow moseyed to the other side of the road and began to crop grass.

Where had the damned thing even come from? Trey saw the answer to that as he climbed back up to the shoulder. A little way up the road, a tree branch had taken out part of the barbed wire fence. Judging from the other leaf trash and sticks strewn across the road, it was evident that last night's storm had been a doozy.

"Well, Bessie, you're about to see a billionaire change a tire." Trey circled around and popped the trunk. Leaning over the ass-end of the car, he shoved his bag aside and lifted the bottom panel of the trunk.

No spare.

"Or maybe not. Damn it."

Somebody would be hearing about that when he got back to his offices, but for now, he'd settle for arranging a tow. At least, that was the plan until he discovered his phone had died somewhere on the flight from Denver to Mississippi. Undeterred, he dug in his bag for a charger. It wasn't in the side pocket as it was supposed to be. He fished around the other pockets, even emptied the main compartment before admitting defeat. He must've left it in his car in Denver.

"Perfect. Looks like I'm walking."

Thankfully, Wishful was only a couple of miles away. He'd have probably been there by now if he hadn't felt compelled to take the scenic route from the airport in Lawley. But he'd wanted a chance to unwind from the flight and get his head on straight. Seemed like it took longer and longer to accomplish that every time he came here to check on his assorted ventures.

Trey thought about finding the cow's owner to let them know their animal was loose, but he didn't see a driveway or a house anywhere. Better to get on into town and arrange for the tow truck. Somebody there would likely know whose land this was and who needed to be notified.

Locking the car, he set out for town, grateful for the mild November weather. There was already snow on the ground in Colorado, but this far below the Mason-Dixon, it felt like Indian summer. At this hour, the locals were already at work, their kids at school, so nobody drove by as he walked. It felt strange to be so wholly disconnected. No texts. No calls. No emails. Nothing but birdsong and sunshine. Trey felt the layers of city start sloughing off and slowed his pace as he reached the outskirts of town and the first smattering of houses. As he took the turn onto Maple Street and cut toward downtown, he felt the years peel away too.

The houses in this part of town were tiny. Boxy little two- and three-bedroom houses built in the sixties. They'd been old and a little worn around the edges when he'd seen them last. In the intervening decades, some had become downright dilapidated. Still, others had been fixed up with fresh paint, new shutters, updated landscaping. Trey imagined most of the occupants were young. Maybe first-time homebuyers. Young couples or single parents. He liked the idea of that—fresh starts, new beginnings. He hadn't been so lucky. This place had been an ending for him.

He almost didn't recognize her house when he saw it. The ugly, sandstone brick had been painted a fresh cream. The front stoop had been expanded, replaced with slate, and the roofline had been extended to make a little porch, held up with thick, cedar beams. It gave the house more presence than the squat square had on its own. The azalea bushes, which had been newly planted last time he saw the place, had grown thick and lush, filling up the flowerbeds all along the front of the house. He imagined, in spring, they'd be a riot of color. A tire swing hung from the branch of an oak tree that had been a mere sapling all those years ago, and a little girl's bike lay abandoned in the front yard, as if its rider had just run inside for a snack. Someone had turned this place into a home.

But it hadn't been her.

Trey didn't know how to feel about that. Since he'd started doing business here in Wishful, he'd avoided this place, just as he'd avoided the woman who'd once lived here. That had been a good call. Standing here now, it was all too easy to get caught up in the storm of old emotions, too easy to look at the old picture window and see the moment his heart had cracked right in two.

He'd been eaten up with worry by the time he'd risked coming here. She should've met him hours before at their designated spot, with everything she needed to start over packed. When she didn't show, he'd feared the worst—that her deadbeat husband had found out and stopped her from leaving. Darkness had hidden Trey as he got out of the car, but it made the drama unfolding through the illuminated window stand out with all the clarity of a movie screen. The woman he loved squaring off with the man who'd made her life hell. Trey had already been on his way up the walk, headed for the door, when her husband kissed her. And she hadn't fought him. She'd wrapped her arms around him, and they'd both *laughed* and smiled—as if relieved that some great crisis had been averted. She'd chosen the prison of her marriage instead of Trey.

The wound had never really healed in all these years. He'd expected the memories to stop having power over him the longer he did business here—a sort of emotional exposure therapy. But everything he felt was as strong and steady as it had been for thirty years. Trey didn't want to think about what that meant.

A car horn beeped.

He turned, expecting to see a minivan or a little compact car waiting to pull into the driveway he was standing in, but instead he found a familiar face.

The brunette in the driver's seat rolled down her window. "I thought that was you! What are you doing out here?"

Reliving the past. Trey stepped toward her. "Hiking to town. I had an unfortunate run-in with a cow on my way in."

Norah arched a brow in question.

"The cow won," he added.

The corners of her mouth twitched. "Careful, Gerald. Your city boy's showing."

"Yeah, yeah. Laugh it up. You haven't exactly turned into a country girl since you moved down here." Norah might've been Mississippian by birth, but she'd come back nearly two years ago from Chicago. "I wound up with a blowout and no spare. Cell phone was dead, so I couldn't call anybody."

"Good lord. Hop in. I'll give you a ride."

He circled around to the passenger side and climbed in.

"I didn't realize you were coming back today," she said.

It hadn't been a planned trip. By rights, he should've been on a flight to London, overseeing the final stages of renovation planning for a new property there, but he'd felt drawn back to Wishful. It seemed he'd been feeling that pull more and more over the past eighteen months. As he'd had a full office suite built at The Babylon, he felt justified in doing some telecommuting. It was as close as he came to rest and relaxation these days.

Trey stretched out in the passenger seat. "I was coming in for your wedding anyway, so I thought I'd come early and work from here until. Particularly once I read your latest proposal."

Norah Burke was one of the most brilliant marketing minds he'd ever known. He'd tried to hire her to run his marketing division at Peyton Consolidated, but she'd ultimately taken a job as Wishful City Planner—after convincing him to invest in assorted projects meant to revitalize the economically-depressed town. She was the reason he'd come to Wishful. Part of the reason. His reasons for being here reached far beyond investment opportunities and into the realm of deeply personal—and possibly foolish. But he kept coming back, kept getting further involved in the affairs of the town. Eventually, he'd have to face the consequences.

"Oh, don't get me started. Cam will murder me

if anything else delays this wedding. I think he and the entire staff of City Hall ganged up to block off the city calendar so we could finally set a date."

"You, my girl, are a workaholic."

She glanced over at him and grinned. "Takes one to know one."

"It is possible I resemble that remark," he admitted. "But everything's all squared away for the big day?"

"It is. You'll get to see the church. I've got to swing by and drop off some paperwork on the way. I hope you don't mind."

"You'll still get me to work faster than walking." He noted more downed limbs as they drove. "Big storm last night?"

"It was, as Cam's grandmother would say, a frog strangler. Lots of wind too. Hush was so freaked out she crawled under the bed and shook the whole thing. I suppose we should be grateful she wasn't howling. I…" Norah trailed off, leaning forward in her seat. "No. Oh, no no no no."

Hearing the alarm in her voice, Trey straightened.

Norah whipped into the small parking lot and skidded to a halt. They both stared at the fifty-foot oak tree sprawled, roots-up, across the church. The weight of the thing had caved in part of the roof and a chunk of the south wall, taking out at least two stained glass windows and letting in God knew how much rain.

"This is your church?" he asked quietly.

In answer, the unflappable, always-in-control woman in the driver's seat burst into tears.

"Agnes Crockett is complaining about that stoplight at Market and Spring Street again."

Mayor Sandra Crawford resisted the urge to bang her head against the desk. That defective stoplight had been the object of more contention…

"What do you want to do about it?" Avery asked.

"Put it on the agenda for the next City Council meeting." It wasn't the first time it had been on there and probably wouldn't be the last. Their town was in considerably better shape financially than it had been, but they had other priorities. Like recovering from the $124,000 their previous city planner had embezzled from city coffers. Sandy still hadn't gotten over the fact that had happened on her watch.

"What's next?"

Her administrative assistant consulted the list in her hands. "You've got a meeting with the Christmas parade planning committee next week to discuss in-case-of-rain plans. And at three o'clock you're meeting with Linda Odom and Beulah Cartwright."

"Why?"

"Well, it seems the Singing Christmas Tree has become the Battle of the Baptists. There isn't enough room for everyone in the stands, so someone has to decide who actually gets that honor—the choir from First Baptist or from St.

Paul Baptist."

"How did that someone get to be me? I'm no music expert."

"No, but you're the boss."

Sandy loved her job—most of the time. Her town meant everything to her. But some days, she felt less like the mayor and more like an over-extended kindergarten teacher. Today was clearly going to be one of those days. "I guess I can't fake food poisoning, can I?"

"Not unless you want to get on Mama Pearl's bad side for impugning the diner's meatloaf."

She'd rather face her ex-husband than insult the Goddess of Gossip herself. That would be the shortest route to historic low approval ratings. "Then I guess I'm putting on my mediator hat. Where are we on reports of damage from last night's storms?"

"A lot of roof stuff. Some downed power lines that Light and Water is already handling. All in all, not nearly as bad as it could've been. Those straight-line winds were killer."

"Let's all be grateful. Is that everything?"

"Just one more for now. Mamie Landon wanted to schedule a time with you to discuss fundraiser options for the Coleman family. They lost everything in the fire last week. The area churches have taken care of the necessities, but there's still the issue of where they're going to live."

That right there was why Sandy loved what she did. Because her town cared about their own. "See if you can schedule that for tomorrow. And while you're at it, check with Brody Jensen and see if you can't get him in as well." Brody was one of her son Cam's best friends. He'd returned to town a year ago and opened his own construction firm. It could be he'd have some ideas about rebuilding and could give them a cost estimate for reconstruction.

"I'm on it."

As Avery rose from the chair across the desk, a knock sounded on the open door. Sandy looked up to find Cam standing in the hall. Her quick spurt of pleasure shifted to a Momdar alert as she caught sight of his face.

"Got a minute?" he asked.

"For you, always."

He murmured a hello to Avery as she passed, then shut the door.

"What's wrong, baby?"

"A tree took out the church."

Sandy blinked at him. "I'm sorry, what?"

"That big old oak got uprooted in the storm and fell on the church. I just came from there. The damage is pretty extensive."

"But…how? The storm wasn't *that* bad…was it?"

"With all the rain we've had the past few weeks, the ground was loose. With those winds…it just went straight on over." Her tall, broad-shouldered son scooped a hand through his blond hair. "Norah cried. She never cries."

Sandy knew that gutted Cam. His fiancée had been a beacon of hope during the darkest hours for their town. If she was shaken, the situation must be worse than dire.

"We've been planning this for months. It took nearly a *year* to pin her down for a date in the first place. How the hell are we going to have a wedding with no venue?"

Her mind was already spinning, considering options. "We'll find a way. I promise." She didn't know what that way was, but she'd find it if only to take that look of dejection off her baby's face.

"I've gotta get back to the nursery—we're rotating some stock for a Thanksgiving sale and Violet wants me to do up some more planters—but I just wanted to swing by and let you know, so you could put your thinking cap on."

Sandy came around her desk and hugged him tight, wondering when he'd started towering over her since he was twelve years old yesterday. "I'll do that. And I'll call Mom. She'll call everybody else. Between the lot of us, we'll figure something out. We've got nearly two weeks."

"It'll take a miracle."

It might take more than that. But Sandy kept the thought to herself as she ushered her son out. When he was gone, she paced a few restless laps in her office. Needing to move, she grabbed her phone and her purse and stepped out into the outer office. "Avery, I'm going for a quick walk. Can you forward my calls, please?"

"Sure thing, Sandra."

She headed down the stairs, her sensible heels echoing off the walls. With a smile and a nod for old Jerry Noble, the security guard manning the front desk, Sandy stepped out of City Hall. She paused for a moment on the steps, soaking in the sight and sound of the town she loved. Courtesy of her future daughter-in-law, Wishful was enjoying its first economic growth in decades. The facelift Norah had arranged to give downtown was in evidence everywhere Sandy looked. Pedestrians strolled the sidewalks and cars lined the streets on all sides of the town green. Her town was not only still alive, it was thriving.

Looking both ways, Sandy crossed Main

Street to the town green. Her destination lay at the far end. Fed by nearby Hope Springs, the fountain dated back to just after the Civil War. And according to local legend, it granted wishes. Norah had rebranded the entire town around it. Banners with their slogan hung from every street lamp that marched the length of Main Street. *Welcome to Wishful, Where Hope Springs Eternal.* She wasn't sure if she really believed. It had been years since she'd made a wish herself and that one hadn't panned out. But because they desperately needed some of that hope if they were going to save Cam and Norah's wedding, Sandy strode purposefully to the fountain.

The happy burble of water was soothing and nice to hear after years of nothing. The temperamental old fountain hadn't run properly since Cam was little, but over the past couple of years, it had slowly been coming back to life. Digging a quarter out of her purse, Sandy held it tight. *I wish for a miracle to save Cam and Norah's wedding.*

She tossed it in, listening to the *thunk* as it hit the water.

Well, that was that. Maybe she should run by Brides and Belles and talk to Babette Wofford. She might have some ideas for alternative, last-minute venues. As she hit the far side of the green and prepared to cross over Spring Street, her phone rang.

"What is it, Avery?" Sandy prayed it wasn't another disaster from the storm.

"You've got a call from Louis Harker over at The Babylon."

She'd seen the name often enough over the past year and a half as the city had begun doing more business with Peyton Consolidated, but generally Norah handled all the liaising. Then again, Norah was supposed to be out for meetings with the Chamber of Commerce this afternoon. "Patch him through."

A moment later, the call connected.

"This is Sandra."

"Mayor Crawford, this is Louis Harker. I'm Gerald Peyton's executive assistant. I'm calling to inquire whether you'd be free for dinner this evening."

It was the last thing she'd expected him to say. "I beg your pardon?"

"With Mr. Peyton," he added. "He has some business he'd like to discuss with you."

Sandy's curiosity piqued. Her town had been doing business with Peyton Consolidated for eighteen months, but she'd never actually met the mysterious Gerald Peyton, III. He was rarely in town, and when he was, he tended to keep to his hotel. According to the local gossip mill, he worked long hours, usually ordering in meals, and rarely actually leaving his offices at The Babylon. All his direct interactions with the city had been handled through Norah, as she was the one who'd convinced him to invest.

"Does Norah need to be in attendance as well?"

"No ma'am. Mr. Peyton was clear this was a meeting specifically for you. Are you available?"

Curiouser and curiouser. "I can be. What time?"

"Seven o'clock. The Spring House."

"I'll be there."

She hung up and her imagination fired. What on Earth could Gerald Peyton want to discuss with her over an after-hours dinner meeting? Especially one without Norah. Did he have some problem with her future daughter-in-law? Was he going to try to hire her away again? Sandy had no idea. But as she prepared for her next meeting, her brain turned to a far more important question.

What did one wear to a business dinner with a billionaire?

CHAPTER 2

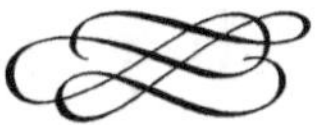

TREY ARRIVED AT THE Spring House early. He told himself it was because he wanted to get out of his office or because he wanted a chance to set the stage, so he'd have the upper hand at this meeting. But he was kidding himself. Nothing about the private little solarium overlooking Hope Springs said *business meeting*. The wine, the candles, the view. They were all trappings of a date. Having Louis set everything up had been yet another delaying tactic, the latest in a long line of them he'd employed in an effort to avoid coming face-to-face with Sandra Crawford since he'd started doing business in her town.

The God's honest truth was that he was nervous for the first time in decades. Peytons didn't get nervous. They made others nervous with their wealth, their prestige, their control. But he'd never been in control when it came to Sandy Crawford.

He had no idea how this dinner would go. He'd spent the past year and a half watching, listening, gathering information on Wishful's two-term mayor. Like him, she was divorced and single. By all accounts, she'd stayed that way since her deadbeat ex-husband had walked out on her and their eleven-year-old son nearly twenty years before. She was tightly enmeshed with her family—what a concept—and the townspeople loved her.

Trey had loved her once.

He'd spent the last eighteen months trying to figure out if he truly still did.

He fidgeted, starting to reach for his phone, then stopping himself. What was the point of having people if he didn't trust them to do their jobs? He employed thousands across the globe. They could get on with running his business without him for one night. But that left his hands empty and his mind too full of questions and possibilities. Maybe he should go find the waitress and order a scotch.

Trey rose, but a motion in the doorway had him freezing in place. The hostess, followed by a tall, willowy blonde, in a little black dress that managed to be both elegant and conservative at once. His heart began to hammer. Would she even recognize him after all these years?

Sandy stepped over the threshold, her heels clacking softly on the brick floor. She was smiling at the hostess. "You be sure and tell your parents I said hello."

Small towns, he thought.

"Yes, ma'am, I will. Your server will be with you shortly. Please enjoy your meal."

The young woman withdrew, and Sandy turned, her step faltering as she caught sight of him, still standing at his seat. Her face went slack with shock, her cheeks going pale beneath her carefully applied makeup. "Trey?" Her smooth voice was barely a whisper.

She remembered him after all.

He worked up a smile. "No one's called me that in a very long time."

They stared at each other, the silence humming with tension and thirty years of unasked questions.

Move your ass, Peyton. Manners saved him as he scooted around the table to pull out her chair. "Please, sit."

For a long moment, Sandy didn't move. Trey wondered if she was just going to turn around and leave again. After all his subterfuge, he wouldn't blame her. But ultimately, she crossed the room and took the seat he offered. As he pushed in her chair, he caught a faint whiff of her perfume or maybe her shampoo—something subtly floral, with notes that reminded him of the sea—and beneath it, a scent that was purely Sandy. He had a ridiculous urge to bury his nose in her hair. Instead, he circled around the table and took his own seat.

Sandy held herself stiff as a board, her expression caught somewhere between discomfort and outright panic. Definitely not the reunion he'd fancied. What must be going through her head right now? A laundry list of all the interactions Peyton Consolidated had conducted with the city government through proxies and representatives? All the times he could've revealed himself and hadn't? Or was she thinking of that last night? Of him waiting for hours at the old Hoka Theater in Oxford?

Trey poured a glass of the Cabernet that had been breathing since his arrival and nudged it toward her. "Here, this will help."

She just shook her head. "I don't understand. You're Gerald Peyton?"

"The third. Hence, Trey, back in college."

"All this time you knew about me, and you said nothing?" There was just a hint of temper beneath the incredulity. Justified.

"No."

"Why?"

He lifted his own glass, buying time. But what else was there to say except the truth? "You made your choice years ago. I was simply honoring it." The tone that came out was the cool one he usually reserved for boardrooms. He needed the cool confidence of the billionaire just now to cover the personal weakness of the man.

Her fingers flexed around the stem of her glass and her cheeks flushed. Shame wiped out her irritation. "What must you think of me for how I handled things?"

She'd left him hanging, never even offering an explanation. And what explanation had he really needed? He'd seen her pick Waylan. He'd known he was beaten and that whatever she felt for him wasn't enough.

Trey twitched his shoulders, restless with the memory that had been too close to the surface since this morning. "You chose someone else. It doesn't matter what I think. And anyway, that's not why I asked you here tonight."

Another faint shake of her head told him she was off-balance. "Then why?"

"I heard about what happened with the church. I want to help make sure Norah and Cam's wedding still happens."

A faint pleat appeared between her brows. "Why would you do that?"

"I was with Norah when she saw the church. I know how much this means to her. She's become something of a surrogate daughter to me over the last couple of years, and I want to see her happy."

Sandy took a long drink of the wine before meeting his eyes. "So why bring me in? Why not just go directly to her? Or to Cam?"

"Because I don't want to tell her until there's actually a plan we know will work. No sense in getting her hopes up if we can't pull it off. And because I didn't think their wedding was the right venue for you to find out about me."

Across the table, she spun her glass between two fingers, eyes fixed on him. "That's very thoughtful of you. On both fronts."

"I'm a thoughtful guy." He meant it as sarcasm.

"I remember that about you. I remember a lot of things about you."

The specter of the past seemed to float between them, a barely acknowledged ghost he didn't want to deal with. He wasn't fool enough to go down this path again. Was he?

The waiter interrupted the weighted silence, reeling off the specials. By the time he scampered off to turn in their orders, Trey had himself under control again. Mostly.

"So, the Babylon is, unfortunately, out. Both the ballroom and the rooftop gardens are booked that day for other functions. I checked as soon as I got in this morning."

She studied him for a long moment, those hazel eyes full of questions. At last she said, "What exactly do you propose?"

"I don't know yet, but we're smart people. I figure between the two of us, we can come up with something." And maybe by the end of this dinner, he'd come up with a way to put these feelings to rest.

SANDRA THANKED God for the fact that it was a Tuesday and the Mudcat Tavern was about to close for the night. That meant fewer prospective witnesses to the stupendous freak out that had been simmering inside her since she'd walked into the solarium at The Spring House. But no, she couldn't think about that. Not yet. As mayor, she had a certain image of control to maintain at all times. Beyond that, she didn't want the inevitable gossip to get back to her family. If she lost it in public, the entire messy clan would hear about it and be after her for explanations she couldn't give.

Only one other living soul knew about her history with Trey, and she currently moved with smooth efficiency behind the U-shaped bar, racking glassware and chatting with her regulars. There weren't many at this hour and none that Sandy knew well enough to speak to. Small blessings. She stepped up to the bar, laying her clutch on the polished wood.

Adele Daly scanned her from head to toe and, with the privilege of long friendship, declared, "You look like crap."

Sandy grimaced. Exactly what you wanted to hear when you'd just shared a meal with your ex, the billionaire. Except Trey Peyton had never been anything so simple as an ex.

"You want a drink?"

No. The one glass of wine had been enough. "I'm driving. Do you have a minute to talk?"

Without hesitation, Adele looked over her shoulder. "Joe, can you come finish this up, please?"

"You got it."

Swapping places with Joe Fowler, her second in command, Adele slipped out from behind the bar and jerked her head toward the kitchen. Sandy followed her back, through the swinging doors, where scents of grease and sizzling beef mixed with the sharp tang of detergent. They kept going, into Adele's little hole of an office, where a battered metal desk, painted fire engine red, was crammed in with a desk chair and a creased leather loveseat. She sank down on the latter as Adele shut the door. Only then did she begin to shake.

Adele dropped onto the sofa beside her, reaching for her hands. "Honey, what's wrong? Is this a hide-a-body kind of crisis? Because I can go get my truck."

Sandy laughed. "No. No truck necessary." Although she was rethinking that drink. Her deep breath did nothing to calm the nerves jumping like a cat on a hot tin roof in her belly. "Have you ever met Gerald Peyton?"

Adele blinked. "The guy who owns The Babylon?"

The boutique hotel and spa was only one of a myriad of projects Peyton Consolidated had its fingers in around town. Norah had recruited him as an investor before she'd even taken on the job of city planner. He had to have known when he signed the memorandum of understanding with the city that Sandy was mayor. Which explained why, since their initial partnership, her future daughter-in-law had been the primary liaison between the company and the city. In a year and a half, the pair of them had done wonders for Wishful's flagging economy. And Sandy had suspected nothing. Resentment prickled.

You made your choice years ago. I was simply honoring it.

She pulled herself back to the conversation. "Yes."

"I don't think a rich real estate mogul has much cause to frequent my bar, especially since his hotel has one of its own. But he did come in for drinks with Brody Jensen once, back when Brody still worked for him. I don't remember much. Dark-hair. Suit. Kept to himself. Why?"

"I had dinner with him tonight."

Adele's blue eyes went blade sharp, her fists automatically curling. "Was he an asshole? Did he get handsy? Because I can get that taken care of, millionaire or no."

She loved Adele for her instant readiness to defend. But she'd never been good at letting others fight her battles. Look at how things had turned out with Trey.

"Billionaire. And no."

"Then what's the problem? What did he say to upset you?"

Sandy clasped her trembling hands around her knees and shook her head. "It's not what he said. It's who he *is.*" She lifted her gaze to Adele's. "It's Trey."

For a long moment, Adele's face was blank. Then comprehension dawned and her hand tightened on Sandy's arm. "Oh. Oh, damn. How did you not know this?"

"I never knew his proper name was Gerald. I didn't know Trey was a nickname because he's a third. And he's gone to a great deal of trouble to avoid any face-to-face time with me since he began investing here."

"So, what, after nearly thirty years, he just up and invites you to dinner?"

"It wasn't about me." Why should that sting

so much? As he'd said, she'd made her choice, though it hadn't been the one he imagined. She'd lived with it.

"Then what the hell was it about?"

"He was with Norah when she found out a tree fell on the church. He wants to help make sure the wedding still happens."

"I heard about that, bless her heart. Mitzi Culpepper was in here, saying it might be some kind of an omen. I set her straight." Adele rose and opened the bottom drawer of the desk, pulling out the top-shelf scotch she kept hidden there for emergencies. "Anyway, that's nice of him and all, but that's not what I really want to hear right now. You haven't seen this guy in thirty years. What was that like? What's *he* like?" She splashed two fingers of the scotch into a low ball and handed it over.

"Still gorgeous." He'd grown from boyish to full manhood. The years looked good on him. But as impressed as she was by the man he'd become, it was the boy she'd seen when she looked at him. The earnest, fiercely protective friend she'd fallen in love with. The one she'd nearly changed everything for.

She couldn't help but wonder how she looked to him. She'd put weight back on since her cancer went into remission, and her hair had grown back. She was acutely aware of every flaw, every imperfection, every year she carried that hadn't been there the last time she'd seen him. "Seeing him again makes me feel both nineteen again and utterly ancient." Like she needed more of a reminder that she was knocking on the back door of fifty.

"So, did you tell him?"

"Tell him?"

"About what really happened with Waylan. Why you didn't meet him that night."

"I was too busy trying not to hyperventilate. And anyway, we didn't talk about the past at all." Not really. "He wanted to talk about the kids."

Adele arched a dark brow. "Are you seriously telling me you spent an hour or more having a meal with this guy and all y'all talked about was Cam and Norah's wedding?"

Sandy shrugged, because reality defied expectation. "He was all business." She'd been very conscious she was having dinner with the billionaire he'd become, not the man she remembered. And yet he'd made arrangements for the chef to prepare a pineapple upside down cheesecake. Just like they used to share at the Hoka back in college. What did that mean?

"So, how are you feeling about all of this?"

She lifted her hands, let them fall. "I hardly know. But seeing him again is stirring up all kinds of feelings I thought were long dead and buried. I put him out of my mind years ago. I had to, to survive things with Waylan." And she hadn't let herself think of Trey after the divorce, hadn't let herself even consider the what ifs or regrets.

"And after Waylan?" Adele prodded.

"I had Cam to raise."

"He's raised now. Thanks to you and the rest

of the clan, he grew into a fine man. So, you don't have him as an excuse anymore."

"An excuse?" Sandy frowned.

"For avoiding men. Don't even deny it."

"Why would I? You've been with me on that train for a very long time."

"Yeah, well, maybe we've done that long enough."

Sandy stared at her. "You can't seriously be saying I should go after Trey Peyton."

"Are you actually letting him help with the kids' wedding?"

"At this point, I'm open to anybody's help to make sure this wedding still happens."

"Then I imagine you're going to be working closely together to pull it off. If you've got unresolved feelings, he may too."

Did he? Sandy wanted to believe there'd been something more than the echo of memory between them, that she wasn't just someone he shared an awkward history with. But he'd been so cool and businesslike. Maybe she was foolish to think that anything he'd felt for her could've survived the past thirty years.

Adele nudged the glass, and Sandy automatically took a sip, wincing at the burn of it down her throat. She never had liked scotch.

"I'm just saying, it's worth exploring, getting some closure, if nothing else."

Closure. Whether Trey felt anything or not, *she* certainly felt something—not the least of which was a bone-deep guilt at how she'd treated him back then. Maybe Adele was right. Maybe she needed to clear the air with him. He had a right to know why she hadn't come. So, she'd tell him the truth and relieve herself of that burden, once and for all. And that would be the end of things between them. Again.

CHAPTER 3

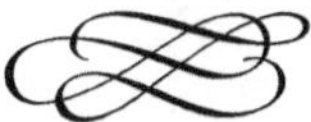

"MAYOR CRAWFORD IS HERE to see you, sir."

Trey absorbed the quick jolt of nerves and pleasure, grateful Louis couldn't see him through the intercom. *Slow down, idiot. She hasn't come for you. This is about the wedding.* But she *had* come instead of just calling or doing something else to re-establish distance between them. He rolled his shoulders and smoothed down his tie. "Send her in."

His door opened. Sandy strode in, offering a

quick, careless smile to Louis—the kind of smile she'd once aimed at him.

Trey tamped down the flicker of jealousy and rose to greet her. "Good morning."

"Morning."

"You want some coffee?" The last thing he needed was more caffeine jittering through his system, but he needed something to do with his hands.

"Sure."

Louis started toward the sideboard, where a coffee service was always set up, but Trey waved him away. "I'll get it."

His executive assistant threw a startled glance in his direction. Trey did not serve people. "Yes, sir. Will there be anything else?"

"Not at the moment. Thanks, Louis."

Then they were alone, Sandy standing in the middle of his penthouse office. Trey wondered what she saw. He poured the coffee, reaching automatically to add one cream, two sugars to hers before realizing he should've asked if that was still how she drank it. He turned to do exactly that and found her staring.

"You have a very good memory."

"We drank a lot of coffee back in college." Endless conversations over warm mugs, in cracked vinyl booths. "Please, have a seat."

She chose an end of the leather sofa. Better than a chair by his desk. Not as good as the middle of the couch.

Reminding himself that this wasn't a date, and he was a grown-ass man who wasn't going to pursue her, he crossed over and handed her the coffee before taking the chair adjacent to her.

"I wanted to bring by the list of everything that's been bought, reserved, or otherwise planned."

"You got all that together since last night?"

She pulled a thick binder out of her briefcase and handed it over. "Please. It's Norah. She has a subdivided, color-coded copy of everything for everyone involved."

He laughed. "She does love her organization.

My daughter does, too. It's part of why I'm so fond of Norah. She reminds me of Tess."

"I didn't realize you had children."

"Just the one. Tess is twenty-six and a total ball-buster, which I hated when she was a teenager, but I admit I kind of love now that she's grown." He waited for the follow-up question about his wife, but it didn't come. Maybe she didn't care. Maybe she really was here just about the wedding. He'd given her no indication that this was anything more. And damn it, it wasn't.

Calling himself an idiot, he flipped open the binder.

Sandy pointed to the first page. "She's got her dress and has already had her final fitting. The bridesmaid dresses are in. The flowers are ordered, and she's deferring to her mother on the cake, as apparently Margaret didn't get to eat any of her own wedding cake, other than the bite for the pictures."

Trey glanced up. "I suppose Joseph was too consumed with working the reception." Norah's father had always been more concerned with appearances than taking care of the people around him.

"Something like that." She angled her head to study him. "You never did like Joseph."

"No." He had no respect for a man who didn't take action when it was called for. Thirty years ago, Joseph Burke had done nothing to control the rowdy freshman pledge under his leadership, and Sandy had paid the price.

Water under the bridge.

Trey continued to flip through the book. "So, it looks like the biggest thing is a new venue for both the ceremony and the reception, then making certain that the new venue for the latter will work with what's set up with the caterers and the florist."

She settled back in her seat, brows faintly raised, studying him.

"What?"

"I just thought you'd hand this over to your staff and let them take care of it."

It was Trey's turn to arch his brows. "Do you think so little of me?"

Her cheeks flushed. "No. I just meant, you're a busy man."

"My schedule is keeping me in town for a while." He'd had Louis arrange it that morning. "And anyway, this isn't about me. It's about them. *I* want to do this. Not my staff."

Sandy shifted, crossing her legs. The motion made her skirt rise up, showing a couple of inches of very excellent legs. She'd always had amazing legs.

"How is it you got to be Gerald?"

Trey made a face. It felt weird—wrong somehow—for her to call him that. He'd never been Gerald with her. That had been part of her appeal. No burden of expectation to live up to the family name.

"When I left Ole Miss, I transferred to the University of Washington. New school, new state, new me. It seemed like it was time for me to grow up."

"I've been trying to reconcile my memory of

you with—well—all this." She gestured to the plush office, the enormous mahogany desk. "I never connected you with Peyton Consolidated. There's no picture of you on your company website, and you've mysteriously managed to stay out of the press."

"You looked me up?" The idea of it pleased him.

"No one does business in my town without my knowing something about them. I wouldn't have agreed to all this on Norah's word alone, though it certainly carries a lot of weight."

"I like my privacy. Keeping my face out of the public eye ensures that I can keep it." He tried to tell himself to leave it there. Surface. Professional. But the lure of the past was too strong. "Am I so different?"

She seemed to consider the question. "You're very at ease in your skin. And there's definitely an aura of power and control you didn't have at twenty. But you're still...Trey."

Something warmed inside him at her words. He rose and poured them each another cup of coffee before crossing to sit beside her on the sofa, close enough he could reach out and touch her. Instead, he handed her the mug and draped his arm along the back of the couch.

"That is the best possible compliment you could've paid me. I haven't been just Trey since college. Since you." A fleeting smile curved his lips and his fingers itched to toy with the ends of her hair. And damn it, he wanted to be Trey right now, not Gerald. Giving in to temptation, and maybe to test them both, he snagged one silky end, rubbing it between his fingers. "I always liked who I was with you best."

Sandy went very still but didn't move away. "Who did you become without me?"

"My father. My grandfather. Someone I didn't recognize. Someone my wife grew to despise."

She balked at that, recoiling a couple of inches. Just far enough to tug the hair from his fingers. "You're still married?"

"Divorced," he assured her. "Rightly so. I was a lousy husband and father. I rectified the latter after the divorce. And Maura and I make much better co-parents than spouses."

"What went wrong in your marriage? Was it just that you were a workaholic?"

Were they going to swap war stories of their divorces now? He knew that was a popular tactic among divorcees, but he'd never been one to participate. Still, he found himself continuing to talk. He'd always been able to talk to Sandy. "I didn't love her. Not the way I should've." The circumstances of their marriage hadn't been the best, but they'd made do. "I thought giving her a lavish lifestyle would make up for that, but it didn't. She deserved better than the likes of me, and she's but one thing on a laundry list of regrets in my life."

You were the biggest.

"There's no sense in focusing on regrets. It's too easy to drown in them. We can't change the past."

Was she speaking generally or about them in particular? He knew which he wanted it to be. "Fair enough. I'd like the chance to prove

I've gained a little wisdom with years." But it wasn't wisdom driving him now. Right now, he wasn't the cool-headed businessman. He was just a boy, sitting beside the girl he'd loved beyond reason.

Keeping his eyes on hers, Trey reached out to take one of the hands resting in her lap. Her fingers were slim and delicate, cold in his, with the barest of tremors. The pulse at the base of her throat fluttered, and her eyes, those lovely hazel eyes that had haunted his dreams, went wide.

"Sandy, I—"

The intercom buzzed and Louis's disembodied voice shattered the moment. "Mr. Peyton, I've got Tokyo on the line for you."

Silently cursing his assistant, his company, and all his responsibilities, Trey struggled to keep his voice level and professional. "Give me just a minute."

Sandy tugged her hand gently free of his and picked up her briefcase. "You're busy. I need to get back to work myself."

"I'll finish going over the details later today." At the very least, he was going to secure another wedding planning meeting with her.

She hesitated. "Why don't we discuss it over dinner. At my house." Her lips curved a little. "Less chance of interruption."

The boy wanted to whoop. The businessman insisted he should say no. That he should do whatever was necessary to get this back on more professional footing.

Trey was tired of being the businessman. "What time?"

"Seven?"

"I'll bring some wine."

"Seven," she repeated, and slipped out his door.

He found himself grinning as he answered the phone. "*Moshi moshi?*"

SANDY ANGSTED over what to do for dinner. What to make. What tone to set. What she actually wanted. God, it had been so long since she'd let herself even think about what *she* wanted. She'd invited Trey on impulse, her nerves still jumping from the look in his eyes as he'd taken her hand. Definitely not business on his mind. That look had given her hope. Though of what she wasn't sure.

He'd been so closed off during dinner. Sandy knew she'd hurt him. Deeply. Under the circumstances, she couldn't really blame him for avoiding her. But, then, why had he come back at all? Why had he chosen to do business here, knowing she was mayor? Norah was persuasive, certainly, but even she wasn't that good. Maybe he just wanted resolution.

Well, she could give him that. Adele was right. He needed to know what really happened all those years ago.

In the end, she opted for casual. His professional accomplishments aside, he was still Trey. Once upon a time, they'd been comfortable together, and it surprised her how much she wanted to be comfortable with him again.

She'd missed their friendship all these years, missed the long conversations and the way he could make her laugh. And she couldn't deny a deep curiosity about how their lives might have turned out if there hadn't been the barrier of her foolish marriage to her high school sweetheart. Because they'd both felt more than friendship. She didn't know what she felt now. Still attracted, that was for damn sure, and that was…intriguing. She couldn't remember the last time she'd been attracted to a man, the last time she'd wanted to make the effort.

She changed clothes three times, while the pork chops were simmering and the carrots were roasting. When she started fussing with her hair, she cursed herself as an idiot and deliberately headed back to the kitchen to start the rice. Unable to sit still, and needing to do something other than stare into a mirror and wonder how she could erase the last thirty years from her face, she set the table, pulling out placemats and cloth napkins, and filling a pitcher with late blooming flowers from her garden.

When the doorbell rang, her heart leapt. Pressing a hand against her chest, she muttered, "It's just dinner." But it felt like more as she opened the door and found Trey on the other side, a bottle of wine and a bouquet of irises in his hands. A messenger bag was slung over one shoulder.

"Hi." Oh hell. Why didn't she sound more confident? She wasn't a shy woman.

Trey's gaze skimmed down her, lingering at her feet. His lips quirked. "I dig the purple toes."

She looked down and realized she was barefoot. Crap. She'd meant to put some kind of shoes back on. Being barefoot felt somehow more intimate. *Well, you wanted casual.* "Please, come in."

"Something smells amazing."

"Pork chops with mushroom gravy."

He held the bottle of wine up. "Sauvignon blanc should be perfect. These are for you."

She accepted the flowers, not bothering to

resist the urge to bury her face in their sweet scent. When was the last time a man other than her son had brought her flowers? Decades. And these had not been picked up at the last second from McSweeny's Market. "Thank you. They're lovely."

He trailed her back to the kitchen. "Ah, already have flowers, I see."

"From my garden." It seemed somehow important to make it clear that there was no one else in the picture.

"So, Cam comes by his green thumb honestly."

Relieved he understood, she retrieved some scissors and began cutting stems, tucking each iris into the pitcher. "He does. He designed an absolute showpiece in the back and put it in for me a few years ago." When she'd been so sick from chemotherapy, she could barely leave the house. "So, I can usually have fresh flowers about ten months out of the year."

"He did an amazing job with the rooftop

gardens at the hotel. I'll have to come back in daylight sometime to see the full effect here."

In daylight. Sometime in the future. Implying he'd be around, for a while at least.

"You will," she agreed.

As she worked, Trey set down the bag and prowled over to the stove, lifting lids and sniffing in appreciation. It looked domestic and comfortable. Sandy waited for the disquiet to come from having someone else in her space besides family but felt none.

"Wine glasses?"

"Upper cabinet to the left of the dishwasher."

She watched him as he pulled them out and utilized the corkscrew she'd left out on the counter. He looked…right there, in her kitchen. And that was utter crazy talk. But for just a moment, she let herself dream. This could have been their life had things been different. Sharing a meal and conversation at the end of the workday. That had never been her reality with Waylan, and no one had tempted her to break her solitude in the years since the divorce. Until now.

"There's something I need to tell you." The words spilled out before she could stop them.

Trey's hands stilled on the bottle. "About?"

Damn it. She'd meant to wait until later, after their dinner and some catch-up conversation. But the truth was burning in her throat, desperate to get out. "That night, thirty years ago."

Something flickered over his face. "Sandy, you don't have to—"

"Yes, I do. Just listen." She flattened her palms on the table to keep them from trembling. "It wasn't what you think."

His lips flattened. "I saw you that night. It was pretty damned clear."

His announcement derailed her train of thought. "You—What? Where?"

"When you didn't show up, I got worried and came to Wishful. To your house. I saw you with Waylan through the window. It was obvious you'd made your choice."

So that was how he'd known. She'd always wondered. Crossing her arms, she cupped her elbows. "You're right. I did choose someone else. I chose my son."

A crease appeared between his brows. "What?"

"I was ready to break things off with Waylan. My bags were packed. I was just waiting on him to get home. I'd been sick as three dogs for days, but I just assumed it was nerves because what we were doing was so huge." Because she'd accepted that her marriage was a failure, and she'd fallen in love with someone else.

"You were pregnant?" By the shock in his tone, it wasn't a possibility that had ever crossed his mind.

It had been the best and worst day of her life.

"I'd found out just that day. The idea hadn't even occurred to me. But my sister-in-law called wanting celebratory Mexican because her morning sickness was finally past and something just clicked in my brain. I didn't think it was possible under the circumstances, but then I was paranoid, and I had to know before I talked to him. And then I couldn't *not* tell him. He was so damned happy, and I didn't know what else to do. I couldn't tell him I was having his child and that I was leaving him in the same breath. And how could I come to you carrying another man's baby? You didn't sign on for that. In the end, it didn't matter. By the time I got free to try to tell you, you were gone, and the decision was made for me."

Trey said nothing and instead poured himself a glass of wine and drained it. Some of the tension seemed to have left his shoulders as he set the glass on the counter with a clink. He met her eyes. "For what it's worth, I'd have gladly taken him as my own."

Her heart squeezed as the implications slid through her. The girl she'd been wanted to cry out in shock and fresh loss. Would it have made a difference if she'd known that? Would she have believed him? It hardly mattered now. She smiled, knowing it was sad around the edges.

"But then you wouldn't have your Tess. And we might neither of us be where we were supposed to be to affect the most good."

He circled around the counter, bringing the wine. "You believe in that? Fate?"

Reaching for the remaining flowers, she considered the question. "I think there's always choice. But there's a right path and a wrong path. And the two can often get confused because what's right isn't always what we want."

He filled the glasses and set the bottle aside. "What does that mean for us now?"

Sandy's mouth went dry, her pulse beginning to drum in her ears as he set the wine aside. "Is there an us now?"

Trey moved in, planting his hands on the table behind her, boxing her in. "I think that, for the first time in thirty years, there's nothing stopping us from finding out."

He was big and warm and inherently male in his dress pants and shirt, the top button popped on his collar, a five o'clock shadow darkening his cheeks. She wanted to rub her hand along the scruff, feel the contrast between the rough stubble and the softness of his hair. All the touch and textures she hadn't allowed herself to explore in college because she hadn't been free.

She expected him to close the gap between them, but he didn't. Instead, he stayed where he was, well inside her personal space, brown eyes steady on hers, waiting. Giving her a chance to acclimate? To change her mind? She couldn't think with him so close. Couldn't figure out what it was he expected. God, she was so out of practice with this.

"You have to choose," he murmured.

He was giving her the choice. Maybe it was for himself. Maybe he needed her to do now what she hadn't done then. But having that power put back into her hands made her all but giddy. So many of the important choices hadn't really been hers. Cam hadn't been a choice. He'd been her reality, her world. Without hesitation, she'd given up the life she'd wanted and built a new one around her son—one that often meant her wants and needs were put last, if they got consideration at all. But, as Adele had pointed out, he was grown now. And for the first time in longer than she cared to remember, she felt like a woman.

Her hand trembled as she lifted it to his chest, splaying it over his heart. She felt the thud of it against her palm, a rapid beat that belied his calm demeanor. That made it easier, somehow, to shift in and take the plunge. Eyes still open, she pressed her mouth to his.

She'd only ever kissed him once before, in a weak, stolen moment, after an admission that should've changed everything. That kiss had been full of desperation and guilt and a terrible need. She felt the shimmer of that same need awakening inside her, with absolutely nothing left to hold it back. Rising to her toes, she pressed closer, sliding her arms up around Trey's neck. A noise rumbled in his chest, and his arms wrapped around her, skimming the length of her spine, fitting her body to his. And, oh, what a body. Beneath the conservative suit, she felt the disciplined muscles of an athlete. The years most definitely hadn't softened…any of him.

It was so very tempting to melt against all that hardness. So, she did, sighing into the kiss, into the heat building between them. She'd known, somewhere deep down, that it would be like this with him. It was why she'd been so ruthlessly careful never to be completely alone with him, never to put herself in a position of temptation. He was tempting her now, stroking his tongue against hers, igniting a five-alarm fire. She could hear the bells.

Wait, that wasn't an alarm, it was…what was it? The doorbell? No, the phone.

Sandy broke the kiss, looking toward the cordless phone on the wall, across the room. Trey bent his head, busying his mouth along the column of her throat, making her shiver.

"I should…God…"

"You should let the answering machine get it." He nipped the tendon above her collarbone and had her knees going weak.

She held on tighter, dropping her head back to give him better access.

A moment later, the machine clicked on. "Sandra, I'm sorry to bother you at home. This is Walt Beringer. We've had a massive water main blow over on Phibbs Street. I've already got my people on it, but we need to get an announcement out. We'll have to shut the water off in that entire quadrant. Call me ASAP."

Sandy dropped her brow to Trey's shoulder and blew out a shuddering breath. "It's not Tokyo but…"

"Duty calls." He released her, skimming a quick hand over her cheek. "Do what needs doing. I'll check on the pork chops." And he strode across the kitchen, as if they hadn't just nearly incinerated the kitchen table.

Still breathless, she put on her mayor's hat, shoved her frustrated arousal aside, and picked up the phone.

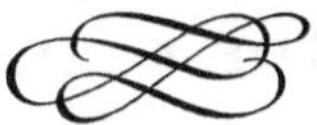

CHAPTER 4

IF THERE WERE MORE appealing scents to start the morning than bacon and coffee, Trey didn't know what they were. The lure of both drew him through the door of Dinner Belles. Even at eight-thirty, the diner was doing brisk business, with three-quarters of the tables still full of patrons nursing plates of pancakes, eggs, sausage, and grits. He could feel his arteries clogging from the smell alone and made a mental note to add a couple of miles to his run tomorrow. Seeing no sign of Sandy, he made a beeline for a booth just being cleared.

After she'd called the water and light department, their tête-à-tête to brainstorm wedding venues—and their unexpected reunion—had been put on hold. They'd had just enough time to inhale the dinner she'd prepared before she had to go in to meet with her people. Hence this morning's breakfast meeting.

The petite brunette, whose name tag read *Hannah*, shot a sunny smile in his direction. "I'll be out of your way in a jiff."

"No rush."

Trey knew from his staff that Dinner Belles was the true hub of Wishful. The latest gossip was served up alongside the finest biscuits and pie in a three-hundred-mile radius, which was why he'd studiously avoided the place since he'd started renovations on his hotel. If he'd set foot in here before now, he would've risked running into Sandy, who was a regular. Although, given how things had turned out last night, maybe that wouldn't have been such a bad thing.

The truth had turned everything he'd believed upside down and stripped away all his reservations. How could he fault her for doing what she thought was best for her son? If he'd waited to talk to her instead of letting his broken heart and wounded pride dictate his actions, would things have turned out differently? No sense in regrets, as she'd said. He couldn't imagine a life without Tess in it. But he'd had no trouble adjusting to the idea of a place in his life for Sandy. He might have buried that dream deep, but in thirty years, he'd never really given it up.

As soon as the booth was cleared, Trey slid in and picked up a menu. The laminated sheet curled at the edges, telling him the choices hadn't changed in years. Combined with the crowd—all shooting curious stares in his direction—that told him the food was damned good. The place reminded him of the greasy spoons he and Sandy had frequented in college. Coffee and studying had given way to talk of life and aspirations. And, eventually, to confidences. He hadn't been able to step into a diner anywhere in the country without thinking of her.

An older African American woman ambled up to the table, radiating sass. "Coffee?"

"Yes, please."

She turned over the cup at his elbow and filled it without looking. "Got tired of take out finally?"

"Beg your pardon?"

"You're the hotel man, aren't you? Always send your people for take out."

"Uh, yes, ma'am." This woman knew who he was?

"That's a sign you work too much."

"Don't we all?" Sandy slid into the opposite side of the booth and beamed a smile. "Good mornin', Mama Pearl."

Ah. Even Trey had heard of Mama Pearl Buckley—Queen of Gossip in Wishful. If Mama Pearl didn't know it, it wasn't worth knowing.

"Mornin', Madam Mayor. You want your

usual?"

"I'm feeling decadent this morning."

Mama Pearl's dark brow lifted a fraction. "Are you now?" She cut her eyes toward Trey as she filled Sandy's cup. "I'll just give you a minute to decide then."

As she disappeared through the kitchen door, Trey released a breath. "Why do I just feel like I was judged and found wanting?"

"Mama Pearl has certain expectations about how life ought to be lived, and she has no problem letting people know when they aren't up to snuff."

"And people are okay with that?"

"She's a wise woman. I may be the political head of Wishful, but Mama Pearl is who really runs this town." She plucked a menu up and scanned it. "Omelet or pancakes?"

"There was a time you would've gotten both."

Her rare dimple flashed, and warmth spread through his chest. "Only because you'd mooch enough off my plate that I didn't feel guilty."

"I can still perform that service."

"Fine. Both it is, then." She tucked the menu back between the napkin dispenser and the condiment caddy.

"Did y'all get the water main squared away?"

"At about two-thirty this morning. I'm sorry about last night."

Trey waved that off. "I get it. Stuff happens. When you're the boss, you have to deal with it. And I'm not crying about getting to share two meals in a row with you." Though he'd have preferred if breakfast had come on the other side of falling into her bed. But that was rushing things.

"Well now," Mama Pearl drawled, dividing a look between them.

Sandy's cheeks pinked. "I'll have a short stack of pancakes and a Denver omelet."

Trey put in his order for biscuits and gravy, with a side of grits and watched Mama Pearl go clip the order to the carousel in the pass-thru window. "That's gonna be all over town by lunch, isn't it?"

"Probably." She winced. "Is that a problem?"

He stretched out to take her hand in his. "Not for me."

Her dimple winked again, and Trey was ridiculously pleased when she curled her fingers around his rather than pull away. Back in college they'd always been so careful never to touch, never to make a wrong move that anybody could misinterpret as more than it was. Having the freedom to touch her now, even something so simple as holding her hand, felt like a gift.

In the back of his mind, cool, cautious Gerald said, *Slow down. Be careful.* But he'd made his decision, hadn't he? To let Trey be in the driver's seat for this. It had been Trey she'd once loved.

"So, what was it you found out this morning?" she asked.

"I met Brody out at the church to assess the damage."

Sandy brightened at the news. "He pulled off a miracle with The Madrigal. What did he say?"

"Well, it's a long-shot, but with enough crew and round the clock shifts like he organized on the theater, he thinks it could be done."

Mama Pearl came back with their food. "Y'all wedding plannin'?"

"We're trying to save Cam and Norah's wedding," Sandy told her.

The older woman nodded. "It's a good cause. Everybody loves those kids. You put out the call, you'll have more volunteers than you can shake a stick at come to help."

Trey loved that about this town. How they'd come together to help their own. He thought there was a nice poeticism to the idea that the town would come together to give back to the couple who'd given so much to it. Between Norah as City Planner and Cam as City Councilman, he couldn't think of anyone other than Sandy herself who'd done more for Wishful. But he had a suspicion that they'd have to go further afield than just the people of Wishful to pull this off.

"Brody's supposed to let me know by day's

end what he needs. I figured we could meet him out there with Cam and Norah and discuss things," Trey suggested.

She beamed. "I think we can make that happen."

And if it meant he got to bookend his day with Sandy, all the better.

BY THE TIME they finished breakfast, it took another twenty minutes to get out of Dinner Belles. One of the side effects of being mayor of a small town was that Sandy knew nearly everyone in some capacity or other, and part of why her approval ratings were so high was because she always took the time to acknowledge that. As she and Trey finally stepped onto the sidewalk, she blew out a breath. "I'm sorry about that."

He only smiled. "I like seeing you in your element. You're a woman in control of your world. It's something I both appreciate and relate to." The smile dialed up to a grin. "And it's sexy as hell."

"Well." Sandy's cheeks burned. He was flirting with her. When was the last time anyone had flirted with her? When was the last time she'd liked it?

Trey tucked her hand through his arm. "C'-mon. I'll walk you back to your office."

On their way across the green, Sandy paused at the fountain, her lips curving.

"What are you smiling about?" he asked.

"I was just musing that I got my wish."

"And what wish would that be?"

"I wished for a miracle to save Cam and No-rah's wedding. Less than a minute later, Louis called, arranging dinner with you."

"How fortuitous." He looped her arm through his again. "You really believe in the legend?"

"Hard to grow up here and not. And Norah's taken local lore and amplified it."

Trey glanced at the fountain. "Hmmm."

"I can hear your skepticism."

His gaze came back to hers, suddenly serious. "Did you ever wish things had turned out differently. Back then?"

Sandy considered her answer. "When things got really bad, I certainly thought about it. But, no, I never made the wish."

"Why?"

"There are all sorts of cautionary tales about being careful what you wish for. Aside from the fact that you can't turn back time, I guess there was a part of me that worried if I made that wish, something might happen to Cam. I wasn't willing to risk it. And I didn't feel like I had the right to be that selfish."

"Selfish how?"

"For all I knew, you'd gone off and built a life somewhere else, were happy with someone else. I hoped you were happy. You deserved the chance for that without me interfering on any kind of theoretical, cosmic level."

She couldn't read his expression. What was going through his head? Did he think her foolish and superstitious?

"Always putting everybody else first." He reached out to tuck a strand of hair behind her ear, letting his hand linger.

Sandy held very still, watching him, though she wanted to turn into the touch. He seemed to have forgotten they were on a public sidewalk, in a town where everyone knew her. But she hadn't. Tongues would be wagging already, and she wasn't in any hurry to give them juicier fodder for the gossip mill.

Trey's mouth curved. "Guess it's my turn to make a wish." He fished a coin out of his pocket. "Any rules to this that I should know?"

"Hold your wish clear in your mind. Don't let your thoughts wander off to something else, or it'll get muddled. And be very careful of your wording, lest you get something you didn't intend."

He nodded, staring at the water for a long moment before tossing in his coin. "Now what?"

"Now you wait."

They began to walk again, this time toward City Hall.

"Want to know what I wished?"

"No! You can't tell. Not until or unless it happens." But she was curious what a man like him, who had everything anyone could ever want, would wish for.

Trey walked her up to her second-floor office, where Avery was neck-deep in spreadsheets for the afternoon's budget meeting with the comptroller. She looked up as they came in, her eyes going wide as she took in Sandy's arm linked through Trey's.

"Good morning Sandra, Mr. Peyton."

"Morning, Avery. Sorry I'm late. Dinner Belles for breakfast."

"Say no more." When the phone rang, she lifted a finger for them to wait. "Mayor Crawford's office. How can I—Yes, she is. Is it ready? No, no, I'll run down and get it." Avery hung up. "Back in a jiff, Sandra. Our order is ready at the print shop."

"I'll hold down the fort."

As her assistant hurried off, Sandy waved Trey into her office. "Welcome to the inner sanctum."

He strode inside and began to look around. She wondered what he thought. She'd done what she could to spruce the place up, bringing in an Aubusson rug and a few pieces of antique furniture she'd picked up at an estate sale, covering the walls with framed black and white photographs of Wishful in its heyday. But there was no hiding the fact that it was a municipal building. He wandered over to the console table set below the bank of windows overlooking the green and picked up a photo.

Nerves had her linking her hands even before he turned. "You have a picture of the Hoka."

"Yes." The old indie theater had been their place. Where they'd hung out. Where they were meant to have met that last night. "I didn't have any pictures of you. Couldn't have kept them if I did. But I had that."

"Sandy."

Trey set the picture aside and crossed to her, sliding his arms around her. It was easy to do the same, to flow into him and lift her mouth to his.

The perfunctory knock on the door had her leaping back as if she'd been scalded—or trying. Trey's grip on her was too firm, so she was still partly in his arms when the older woman with silver hair came into the room.

"Sandy, sorry to bother you, but Avery isn't—Oh, excuse me. I didn't mean to interrupt a…meeting."

Not sorry enough to step into the hall until it was finished, Sandy noted. She moved away from Trey, deliberately not looking at him.

"It's fine, Mom. What are you doing here?"

"I brought you some cheese straws." Helen came all the way into the room, a cookie tin extended.

Sandy took it automatically, frowning as she opened to check the contents. "Cheese straws?" Why was she bringing by cheese straws at nine-thirty on a Thursday morning?

"Well, I'm tinkering with the recipe. Trying out a pimento cheese variety. I thought you'd like to try them out. Go ahead. Have a bite."

"May I?" Trey asked.

Sandy held out the tin, knowing her cheeks were on fire again. It was ridiculous to feel as if she'd been caught at something. She and Trey were both grown adults, both single. But knowing that did nothing to stem the trepidation.

He popped a cheese straw in his mouth and groaned in appreciation. The sound just made Sandy blush harder. He'd made the same sound when she'd kissed him last night.

"I don't know what the originals taste like, but these are top notch. I can't remember the last time I had cheese straws." He plucked one more up before Sandy could close the container.

"And who might you be, young man?"

Trey held out his hand. "Gerald Peyton. Nice to meet you, ma'am."

"Helen Campbell." She shook once, keeping

hold of his hand and giving him a shrewd onceover. "You've been doing a great deal in our town."

"Yes, ma'am."

Helen divided a look between them. "You had dinner with my daughter. And breakfast."

Trey lost some of his cool as shock rippled over his features.

Welcome to small towns.

"Uh, yes, ma'am."

"Just what are your intentions?"

"Mom!" Mortified, Sandy stepped between them.

"What? It's a reasonable question."

"It is not. I'm forty-nine years old."

Entirely unrepentant, Helen reached up to tap her cheek. "And still my baby."

That was it. Sandy was just going to die of embarrassment on the spot. The end.

"To answer your question, I intend to enjoy the pleasure of her company, for however long she's willing to bestow it."

"Hmm. A pretty talker and polite. Norah

speaks very highly of you, so that's in your favor. Perhaps you'll do."

"Mother, that's enough."

Helen just beamed at the warning tone. "I'll go on and get out of your way." She wiggled her fingers. "Tootles." Then she was gone.

Sandy leaned back against her desk because her legs weren't entirely steady. "God. I'm sorry."

"Our fault for not locking the door. How did she even know?"

"Small town, remember. I picked up the pork chops at McSweeney's on my way home last night. Your car was then seen in my driveway."

The CIA had nothing on the gossip network in Wishful.

Obviously amused, he leaned beside her on the desk. "I run a multi-national company that frequently deals with high-level government officials. I can handle meeting your mother."

"It's not just my mother I'm worried about. As soon as the news circulates, I fully expect you to end up hearing from practically every member of my family. We are *adults,* for God's sake." She scooped a hand through her hair.

He wrapped an arm around her shoulder and pressed a kiss to her cheek. "I'm a big boy. I'll survive. Whatever they dish out, you're absolutely worth it."

"Yeah, well, hold on to that thought."

He studied her. "You're legitimately worried about this."

"Yeah."

"Why? What's this really about?"

Sandy held up her hands, let them fall. "It's just…I haven't done this since my divorce."

"Done what?"

"Dated. Not really."

After the disaster of her marriage, her family had felt plenty free to opine about the men she had deigned to go out with. She clearly couldn't be trusted to make a sensible decision on that front, so they felt the need to investigate the candidates and vet them. It hardly made for an environment conducive to forming real relationships. So, she just hadn't bothered. And maybe, on some level, she'd believed them.

Trey stared at her. "You haven't dated in eighteen years?"

God, it sounded even worse when he said it. "My focus was on Cam. Then going back to grad school. And then…there just wasn't anyone who interested me for longer than a dinner or two." And during the years of her cancer, men had been the last thing on her mind.

He didn't try to minimize it. Instead he curled his hands around the desk, his fingers just brushing hers. "I haven't dated much either."

Sandy shot him a look. He was a vital, attractive man. "I find that hard to believe."

"It's not that there wasn't opportunity. It's just…hard to date in my position."

"Your position?"

"Well, to be frank, it's often hard to tell whether a woman is interested in me or in my money."

"Oh." She paused, thinking back to college. "Is that why you never mentioned what you came from when we were at Ole Miss?"

He shrugged. "I was tired of not being judged for who I actually am."

"Understandable." Sandy wished she didn't know about the money now. She wanted to think it didn't make her see him differently, but it did. He didn't flaunt it, didn't announce it, but the fact of his wealth was there, hanging out at the periphery of her mind, reminding her that they came from two different worlds.

It had been easier in college to imagine that they could have a future. To dream up the life they could create together. Now…

Sandy shook off the thought. Now they were enjoying each other's company, getting to know each other all over again. Thoughts of futures and a life were getting light years ahead of things. Right now, she was just going to enjoy the ride.

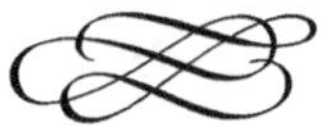

CHAPTER 5

ET ME TO THE church on time.

Trey's eye began to twitch as he watched the clock creep closer and closer to when he needed to leave, while his business associate on video conference continued to drone on about some staffing problems with their new London project. Edward was so damned long-winded. Trey wasn't even sure he'd stopped for breath for the past ten minutes. Maybe he had a future in filibusting. When it became apparent there wasn't a chance he'd get out the door on time, he sent a text to

Sandy.

Gonna be late. Tied up in a meeting. Meet you there?

Her answer came back moments later. **Got it covered.**

What did that mean? Did she not want him to come? He stared at the three little dots that said she was typing more.

Dinner after?

He grinned. At least until he remembered the proposal he had to get through tonight. He'd let a few things slide the last couple of days, but he really needed to get back on track.

Trey: **I want to say yes, but I've got some work tonight.**

Sandy: **So do I. Want to pick up a pizza and bring your homework over?**

The grin came back full-force. This felt like college all over again. Except now there was the possibility of necking on the couch when they were through.

"Gerald?"

Trey snapped his attention back to the video conference. "Sorry. What?"

"I asked what you thought of the projections."

He hadn't even looked at the projections. "I'm still digesting them."

"It's pretty clear-cut." Edward frowned. "Is everything all right? You seem…not yourself."

"I'm just dealing with some personal things." *Like having a personal life.* "Listen, I'm sorry. Can we wrap this up? I have another appointment I'm going to be late for."

Mouth pinched with disapproval, Edward said, "We have to move on this soon or we could run into problems with the permits. That could mean serious delays, and delays cost."

Damn, Trey missed having Brody to deal with this shit. Not that his replacement wasn't qualified, but he didn't have Brody's years of experience. "I swear I'll look it over tonight and get back to you tomorrow."

It took another fifteen minutes to get off the call, and Trey had to get borderline rude to manage it, but eventually he signed off and headed for the church.

Since yesterday, someone had gotten busy with chainsaws and removed the tree from the building. The hole was covered with a series of tarps that flapped in the evening breeze. Trey parked beside Brody's truck and headed inside. Following the murmur of voices, he stepped around the open door and into the damaged sanctuary. Someone had strung caution tape to block off the entire left side of the church. Besides the tree itself, it didn't appear the debris had been moved. And there was an astounding lot of debris—from the overturned pews all the way up to the splintered beams that arched along the vaulted ceiling. Brody had his work cut out for him.

Sandy stood with Brody at the altar, deep in conversation. The overhead light cast a halo on her blonde hair, which she'd bundled into some kind of messy knot since this morning. She'd always been beautiful, but as Trey approached, it struck him that she'd settled into herself and found a confidence that was truly stunning.

Sandy's gaze swung toward him as he approached. "I do."

The longing hit him square in the chest. *Me too.* Trey's stride hitched, just a little at the thought. Oh yeah, he had it bad.

"What's going on?"

"Brody's got concerns."

The younger man spoke up. "I'm not sure I can round up enough qualified people or get the materials in time to pull this off. My crew is largely tied up on other jobs at the moment."

"How many do you need?" Trey asked.

Brody named a figure.

"Done. Anybody in particular you want?"

One dark brow winged up. "Morales and Jacobsen would be excellent crew leaders and allow us to break the whole thing up into three shifts for round the clock project management."

"I'll get them here."

"But what about whatever projects they're on? I don't want to cause you delays."

"It's no problem. And whatever supplies you'll need, we'll get—even if we have to fly something in. Just let Louis know."

"I'm not sure something like that is in the church's budget," Sandy interjected. Her tone said it definitely wasn't.

"I've got it covered," Trey promised. Something like this was a drop in the bucket.

She frowned. "But it's not your financial responsibility."

"It's a tax deduction and a goodwill gesture toward the community. That's good business," he assured her.

"You might as well let him," Brody told her, his lips curving into a smile. "Once he gets the bit between his teeth, there's no swaying him."

"We're settled, then," Trey declared.

"What's settled?" a voice called from the back of the sanctuary. Norah strode up the aisle, hand linked with Cam's.

"The plan for repairing the church."

Sandy stepped forward to hug them both. "Gerald and Brody are making arrangements for all the necessary supplies and manpower to see that it's done in time for your wedding."

"You know it's in just over a week, right?" Cam asked.

"It's a tight timeline, but not the worst I've ever faced," Brody said.

"I'll see that he's got whatever he needs to make it happen," Trey added.

Norah's eyes went suspiciously glassy. "You'd do that for us?"

Trey twitched his shoulders, praying she didn't cry again. "I know it was partly my fault you had trouble setting a date in the first place, because I kept you busy with projects. This seems like the least I can do."

He staggered a bit as Norah threw her arms around him in a tight hug. "Thank you."

The momentary discomfort bled into something warm and fuzzy that had him missing Tess. Trey hugged Norah back, not quite resisting the urge to run a hand down her hair, as he would with his own daughter. "You're most welcome."

Cam offered his hand for a hearty shake. "I don't know how to thank you."

"Really. No thanks necessary. I just hope my own daughter someday winds up with a guy I can like and respect as much as you."

As they turned to offer their thanks to Brody, Trey stepped to the side and called Louis to get the ball rolling. By the time he finished the call, Sandy was pacing back and forth in front of the groom's side of the church, in animated discussion with someone herself, and the kids had migrated to the vestibule. One hand rubbed absently at her shoulder as she spoke. Trey crossed to her and took over, kneading at the knot there. After one, quick jolt, she relaxed into his touch.

She worked so hard. He understood and appreciated that kind of drive, but he wondered when the last time was she'd had a break. When had he? The kernel of a plan began to form in the back of his mind—a means of both impressing her and relaxing them both. But if he was going to pull it off, he had a lot of details to attend to.

"Sorry about that. Still dealing with the aftermath of the storm in a few other areas."

"No problem." He continued to massage her shoulders, loving the faint little whimper she made as she leaned into him.

"I should call in the pizza," she murmured. "Still sausage and mushroom?"

He wasn't the only one who remembered. "Yep." Before she could lift the phone again, he said, "Listen, can you clear your schedule tomorrow night? I want to take you out."

"Four meals in even fewer days? People will talk." But her dimple flashed, so he didn't think she minded too much.

"Not here, for what it's worth," he added.

She looked over her shoulder, equal parts wariness and intrigue in her eyes. "Then where?"

He grinned. "It's a surprise."

"'It's a surprise.' Why do men think that's a good thing?" Sandy demanded. "I don't know where we're going. How am I supposed to know what to wear?"

"It is a mystery for the ages," Adele agreed. But she was grinning.

Sandy scowled at her. "You're not helping."

"I'm sorry, it's just funny. You haven't been this angsty over a date since our sophomore year of high school."

"I'm so glad I can be a source of amusement." She yanked a pair of slacks and some jeans from the closet, tossing both on the bed beside a skirt and one of her dresses. He could have at least had the courtesy to tell her if it was casual or dressy.

"You could always take a really big purse and a change of clothes."

"Because that sends the right message."

"What?" Adele asked. "You want to sleep with him."

"Not tonight!"

Her friend just arched a brow. "I didn't realize there was a requisite time stamp. Does attraction have a maturation date? Like wine or champagne?"

"Oh, don't be ridiculous."

"What's bothering you here? The idea that he might expect you to sleep with him—in which case, he's not the guy you've been describing—or how easy it would be to fall into bed with him?"

Sandy knotted her hands in the sweater she held. "It just feels so fast. All of this feels so fast." She didn't want anyone accusing her of being reckless again.

"Thirty years is fast?" Adele's smirk made irritation prickle.

"We aren't in college anymore."

"No, but you're still fundamentally the same people. If you'd been free back then, would you have slept with him?"

That wasn't even a question. She wished it was. "Yes."

"Okay then. It seems like the last three decades were a really long intermission to something that was inevitable. You're a grown woman, who's free to make her own decisions."

"I'm not arguing that. But say I go to bed with him. Then what? He owns a multi-*billion*-dollar company. His life isn't here in any permanent way. And mine can't be anywhere else." It was the thing that had been circling around her brain all day. How could they have anything permanent with lives so different? And was it worth having him only for a little while? If she let herself get that deep, could she survive losing him again?

"I seem to recall that Norah had the exact same struggle with Cam. And whose wedding are you currently saving? She wanted it bad enough to make a way."

That was unarguably true. Her future daughter-in-law had moved heaven and earth to find a way to be with Cam. But... "She's also not yet thirty and was at a transition point in her life."

"Honey, as you've just pointed out, Trey's a billionaire. He can do whatever he damn well pleases. Now, stop fast-forwarding to an end before you've even begun." Adele gave Sandy a quick, hard hug. "Go to bed with him tonight or don't. That's up to you. But wear those slacks and the green cashmere sweater and pack the jersey dress in your purse, just in case you need to step it up a bit. And wear your good underwear. Whether he sees it or not, it'll make you feel better."

In the end, she wore a dress. At the heart, she was a Southern woman. Everybody knew it was better to be overdressed than underdressed. Even if they ended up at a hole-in-the-wall, like The Beacon, she'd feel more confident looking her best. And hell, he'd said somewhere other than Wishful. Maybe he *was* taking her to Oxford to some of their old haunts.

The khaki pants and button-down shirt he was wearing when he picked her up gave absolutely no additional clues.

"Is this okay?" she asked, brushing at the skirt to smooth imaginary wrinkles.

"You look beautiful." He leaned in to kiss her cheek.

"But is it appropriate for where we're going?"

The corner of Trey's mouth twitched. "It's an anything goes sort of place. You'll be just fine."

Sandy picked up her purse. "You're seriously not going to tell me where we're going?"

"Nope." He laced his fingers with hers and brought her hand to his lips. "I told you, it's a surprise. C'mon."

She hesitated when he opened the door to the back seat.

"Louis is driving us," Trey explained.

And that just elevated this whole date to… something new. They were being chauffeured? Sandy slid into the car and nodded to the stone-faced man in the driver's seat. "Hi, Louis."

"Ms. Crawford."

"Do you know where we're going?"

His eyes met hers in the rear-view mirror,

and she could've sworn she saw a spark of humor. "I'm not at liberty to say, ma'am."

Trey slid in beside her. "He's too well-trained to reveal my secrets. But you're welcome to keep guessing on the way."

Since it felt like a game, she did. She ran through everywhere she could ever remember going with him and quite a few restaurants in Lawley, the county seat about forty miles away. But when they turned down a country road, she knew that wasn't their final destination. This road led…nowhere.

Sandy shot Trey the side eye. "What are you up to?"

"Nothing. Yet. But give me ten minutes." After that cryptic remark, he said nothing else.

So, she lapsed into silence and watched the woods and fields roll by, while he idly played with her fingers, as if he couldn't bear not to touch her. She liked it. She liked all of this more than she should.

"Ah, we're here." Trey leaned forward as they broke free of a stand of trees at…a helipad?

Sandy couldn't even care if she looked like a rube as she pressed her nose to the glass and stared at the tidy little helicopter parked in front of them. "Since when is there a helipad in Wachoxee County? And how did I not know about it?"

"Since I had one put in after I started construction on The Babylon. It's often more convenient to fly than drive. C'mon."

Sandy accepted his hand up out of the car. "Where's the pilot?"

"Right here." He tapped his own chest.

"You can fly a helicopter?" She looked at Louis to see if she was being teased.

"He's been flying for fifteen years, ma'am."

"Well, as dates go, this one is definitely thinking outside the box," she muttered.

"Oh, this isn't what we're doing. This just gets us the first leg of the way. We can get to Lawley in about fifteen minutes by air."

Trey had a helicopter. That he could fly himself. Sandy was still trying to wrap her brain around that, as he took a bag from Louis and led her toward the chopper. Once they were both strapped in, he handed her a headset.

"Just lean on back and enjoy yourself."

Sandy didn't talk on the short flight to Lawley. She didn't want to do anything to distract Trey from what he was doing, and anyway, she was too busy staring at the view below. Her town was so *tiny*. Talk about a perspective check. Her entire *world* was microscopic compared to his. She didn't doubt the importance of her job or her role in the community at large, but he probably employed more people worldwide than the entire population of Wishful.

They landed at a part of the Lawley airport she'd never seen. Not that there was much to the Lawley airport. It was a hub for commuter flights to Jackson, Atlanta, and Memphis. And apparently, today it was hosting Trey's private jet. A sleek little plane, with the logo for Peyton Consolidated painted on the tail, waited on the tarmac, stairs unfolded, staff already waiting to usher them inside. Sandy could only stare.

Trey took her arm. "You okay?"

"I'm just…a little staggered." She was more than staggered. She was intimidated. Back in college, he'd never said a word about his family's wealth. A good thing. She doubted she'd have been able to relax enough around him to get to know who he really was. He'd built on that foundation exponentially in the decades since. Seeing clear evidence of that made it harder to reconcile this man with the boy she'd known.

He grinned at her—boyish and charming—and some of the knots unraveled. "I thought for tonight, I'd go for shock and awe."

He was certainly succeeding. "Are you flying this, too?"

He laughed. "No. I conduct too much business en route to pilot myself. And for the next few hours, I want to focus on you."

Hours? Really, where the hell was he taking her?

Trey led her up the stairs and introduced her to the flight attendant—Imogene Glasner—and the pilot—Jon Beale—before taking her back into the plush cabin. The seats were leather and spacious. There was a bar, where champagne chilled in a bucket of ice. A flat screen TV was mounted on one wall. There was even a *sofa* in the back.

The pre-flight check was a blur. Sandy found herself buckled in and accepting a glass of champagne from Imogene, numbly thanking the other woman.

Trey lost a little of his grin as he took a good look at her. "You're not afraid to fly, are you?"

"No." It was all she could manage.

He slipped his hand in hers, as Imogene disappeared into the cockpit for takeoff. "What's wrong?"

"Nothing."

His thumb stroked across the back of her hand. "Sandy. You've hardly said two words since we left Wishful."

"I...it's just. This is all so...much. I never even dreamed of something like this. I haven't traveled all that much. I was a mother, then a single parent, then mayor. There's just never been a chance." That had never seemed to matter before. But being in his world made her feel small and inexperienced.

Trey brought her hand to his lips again as they left the ground. "I know. I wanted to give you some of what you had to miss. There's no pressure here. No expectation. Just enjoy it."

She looked into his eyes and found him a smile. "I'd enjoy it more if I knew where we were going."

"Nope. Not gonna happen. I'm sticking to my guns that this is a surprise."

Deciding she'd better embrace the concept, Sandy settled back into her seat and sipped the champagne. "Then you, sir, had better keep me entertained."

CHAPTER 6

TREY WAS HAVING THE best dream. An entire weekend of wining, dining, and dancing with Sandy. No work, no worries—just her. The whole thing took a sharp left into the realm of weird when Elvis showed up and started singing a slightly off-key rendition of "Love Me Tender," but who was he to complain? The guy made her laugh. She didn't do that enough. Then the dream bled into an erotic montage that made his body tighten with need. Trey tried to cling to it, to burrow deeper into sleep so he could get to the end, but a pulsing pain in his skull dragged him inexorably back to consciousness.

The dull thump of agony in his head made him want to whimper. Okay, there was *a lot* of champagne last night. He hadn't felt this hung over since…well, he couldn't remember when. As a rule, he rarely overindulged. He didn't like being out of control. Careful to remain utterly still, lest his brain decide to conga right out of his skull, Trey cracked one eye open. His bleary vision resolved itself to a dim room. Just enough light seeped in around blackout curtains that he could tell this wasn't his suite at The Babylon. Where the hell was he? Turning his head just a little, he managed to catch sight of an enormous chandelier above the bed.

Vegas. He was at his hotel in Vegas.

A faint groan beside him had Trey going instantly on alert, hangover be damned. He wasn't alone. With painstaking slowness, he turned his head and saw the tumbled blonde hair, the slope of bare shoulder with a birthmark shaped like a butterfly. He felt an immediate urge to press a kiss there and had a flash of memory that he'd done just that, as he peeled off Sandy's dress the night before. Why couldn't he remember the rest of the night? Nights? What day was it?

He reached out to stroke a hand down Sandy's arm. She rolled into him, nuzzling against his throat and making him excruciatingly aware of the fact that they were both very, very naked. She smelled of him—of sweat and sex and that curious, soft scent of sleep. Well, now he really wished he knew how they'd gotten here.

Something gleamed faintly in the space between them. Tipping his head down, Trey noted a gold band on the hand she pressed against his chest. Frowning, he peered closer. Had she been wearing that when they left Wishful? No, he'd have noticed. Still puzzling over that, he pulled her closer—and saw the matching band on his own left hand.

Uh-oh.

"Sandy." His voice came out like gravel.

"Mmm?" Her eyes blinked open. "Trey?" After a long moment, her bleary expression cleared and her eyes popped wide, her body going stiff. "Trey." She promptly winced, squeezing her eyes shut again as she dragged the covers up to her chest. "My head. What happened?"

Trey had a moment of regret that he couldn't remember what she was hiding beneath that sheet.

"I think, possibly, we drank half the champagne in the state of Nevada."

She squinted at him, as if maybe she was hoping he wasn't real. "And we…um." The wave of her hand seemed to encompass all the nakedness and what had inevitably come before.

"Seems we did. Probably repeatedly, although I'm pretty fuzzy on that point." And that was a damned shame. After waiting thirty years to make love to this woman, he resented the hell out of not being able to remember it.

The flush began at her hairline and swept

down her throat and the chest that was pressed so tantalizingly to his. "I'm pretty fuzzy on all of it."

At least he wasn't the only one.

"You don't happen to remember getting these, do you?" He held up his hand where she could see the ring.

Sandy frowned, lifting her own hand and staring at it like it was an alien appendage. "What?"

"I think…we got married last night."

She started to shake her head, then seemed to think better of it. "Don't be ridiculous. Why would we do that?"

Trey struggled to sift through his patchy memory. "I seem to recall something about thirty years apart being quite enough and announcing I never wanted to let you go." He really hoped the drunken rendition of Sergio Mendes' "Never Gonna Let You Go" was just a dream.

"We can't be married."

"Well, we are in Vegas, and we're wearing

wedding bands we didn't have when we got here, so I'm thinking maybe we can."

Sandy sat up, still clutching the sheet to her chest. "We can't be married," she repeated, panic underscoring her words. "I did not come to Las Vegas for the first time and get married by Elvis. I'm not that irresponsible."

"Was Elvis real? I thought he was just part of my dream."

"Oh God!" She rolled out of bed, dragging the sheet with her as she began to pace. "How did this happen?"

As it seemed highly unlikely he was going to talk her back into bed for a reprisal of the wedding night that was currently a blank, Trey reached for the pants puddled in the floor. He slipped them on and strode past her to the bar in the other part of the suite, pouring them both glasses of water. Stepping into her path, he stopped her frenetic pacing and pressed one into her hand. "Drink."

"What are we going to do?"

Her face was wan and a little puffy from

lack of sleep, and her hair was an absolute wreck. And she was, improbably, his. At last. It felt like every cell in his body began to grin at once—at least, all the ones not currently protesting his status as one of the living.

"Why are you *smiling?*" she demanded.

"Because this is one of my college fantasies fulfilled."

"Getting drunk and married in Vegas?" Incredulity dripped from every word.

Trey set his glass aside and took her face between his palms. "No. Marrying you."

Rather than melting as he'd hoped, she gave him a hard stare. "Did you bring me out here for this?"

He absorbed the insult of that. She was justifiably upset, hung over, and seemed to be just as unclear on the particulars as he was. But how could she even think for a moment that he'd deliberately liquor her up and marry her? "No. I didn't plan on this. I can assure you, if this were on purpose, we'd both have been sober enough to remember all of it. And I'd have employed considerably more thought to the event than pulling you into the nearest quickie wedding chapel." If Elvis had officiated, Trey assumed that's what had happened.

Sandy pulled away and began pacing again, her movements jerky enough to slosh water from the glass. She was too busy babbling to notice. "—an impossible situation. We can't be married. You're involved in a ton of city projects. I'm the mayor. That's a serious conflict of interest that needs to be disclosed. But we can't disclose it. That would take the focus off Cam and Norah, and their wedding is in a week! It *has* to go off without a hitch. And it would be crazy to stay married. We've barely seen each other in thirty years."

Obviously, they'd seen a great deal of each other last night. He wished he could remember more of it. Maybe when the rest of the champagne wore off.

She was still rolling. "But we can't get a divorce either. Nevada requires a six-week residency for a quickie divorce, and neither of us has time for that."

"How do you even know that?"

"Adele did it. And we can't do it in Wishful. That's a formal, public legal proceeding, with a judge that has to sign off on it. Everyone knows me. Which, again would take the focus off Cam and Norah. And dear God, people will think I'm flighty and impulsive. Nobody wants those qualities in a mayor."

He crossed to where she was digging in her purse, gently taking her by the shoulders. "Sandy, we'll figure this out."

"Figure it out? Figure it *out?* Trey, we *got married!*"

From where he was standing, that wasn't a bad thing. He was working on not being offended that she wasn't as happy about it as he was. He hadn't planned to rush her into anything, but he'd have been lying if he said marriage wasn't his end-game with her. He loved this woman. He always had.

Sandy was obviously not in the right frame

of mind to talk about it right now. She was staring at the screen of her phone, her cheeks going pale.

"What?"

"It's Sunday," she whispered. "We've been gone for two days."

"Are you under some kind of curfew?"

With a glare, she snapped on the nearest light, blinding him and sending a fresh bolt of agony into his brain. "It is *Sunday*. I have missed church *and* Sunday dinner with my *entire family*. I have fifteen missed calls. We'll be lucky if my brothers haven't called the police to report me missing. And even if they didn't call out a search party, I still have to find some kind of explanation for where I've been. An explanation I will no doubt have to deliver, in person, to a small army waiting on my doorstep when I get home."

Okay, so that didn't exactly sound appealing. If they were very, *very* lucky, maybe they'd both be over their hangovers by then. And maybe they'd remember some more of the past thirty-six hours.

"We'll deal with it," he promised. "First things first, we need to get back to Wishful. We'll clean up, get some food and painkillers, a fresh change of clothes, and we'll face them down together."

"We can't *tell* them." She looked aghast at the very idea.

"No. We can't," he agreed. Because a drunk, quickie wedding on The Strip was hardly the route to endearing himself to the Campbell clan. Sandy deserved better. A real wedding. Proper rings. To be cherished, as Waylan had never cherished her. "We'll figure it out on the flight home. I'll go call my pilot. Make a call or send a text to your family to let them know you're not dead in a ditch somewhere."

Trey began searching for his cell phone, a task made infinitely easier when it began to ring. He unearthed it from a potted palm in the corner and answered. "Peyton."

"Sir, I'm sorry to bother you, but there's a problem with the London project."

Just the sound of that had his headache cranking up to eleven. He listened, pacing, as Louis outlined the issue. Loss of oversight. Delays. Projected additional costs. Exactly what Edward had warned him of. It was a prospective cluster-fuck, one he needed to wade in himself to sort out.

"I realize you wanted your schedule cleared, but this is time-sensitive. Shall I make travel arrangements?"

"I'm sure as hell not leaving for London tonight. It'll keep until tomorrow." He wasn't leaving town with things such a mess with his new wife. Hell, he hadn't even gotten her back to town.

Louis was quiet for a beat too long. "Yes, sir. I'll see you in the morning."

Trey hung up and turned to find Sandy standing in the doorway to the bedroom, arms folded over her middle. She'd put her dress back on.

"London?"

"It will get handled." He was far more worried about her. Lines of strain fanned out from her eyes and pain pinched her mouth. No doubt her head was pounding as much as his was. Because he couldn't resist, he wrapped his arms around her, pressing a gentle kiss to her brow. "Everything will work out. Without having to search out the nearest means of filing for divorce." He'd make her see that this could be a good thing. A great thing, if only she'd give it a chance.

She sucked in a breath and stepped back, putting more than physical distance between them. "Trey, our lives are incompatible. I'm tied to Wishful. You're due in London tomorrow. A marriage with us could never work."

"London is temporary." He could straighten things out within the week, then be back in time for the wedding.

"And after that, it will be something, somewhere else. Your life isn't in Mississippi."

Okay, point to her, but he hadn't even had

coffee yet. He'd hardly had time to make any life changes. Other than acquiring a new wife. "I realize we haven't figured everything out yet, but I l—"

"What is there to figure out? Do we have feelings for each other? Yes. But they aren't enough to overcome the practicalities."

I love you.

The words froze on the tip of his tongue. Because she was saying love wasn't enough. Not that she had let him get that part out. "You seem to be in an awfully big hurry to say goodbye."

She shook her head, a few tears escaping to slide down her cheek. "I've already used up my lifetime quota of mistakes, Trey. I can't afford another."

"We aren't a mistake," he growled. "And I'm sure as fuck not Waylan."

"Of course not. But I won't settle for a part-time relationship. Not even for you. I've had that, and I'm worth more. And I certainly won't ask you to change your whole life because of one drunken decision."

He wanted her to ask. He wanted her to want him enough to ask for everything. But he didn't say that because he felt too raw and exposed and he was too afraid she'd crush him.

This was way too much to cope with on top of a hangover from hell.

"Let me call my pilot and make arrangements to get us home."

And maybe by the time they landed, he'd have figured out how to convince her that marrying him hadn't been a mistake.

"LET it never be said that I don't love you," Adele announced as she let herself into the kitchen.

Sandy just breathed, "Bless you." How was it possible she felt worse today than she had when she woke up in Vegas yesterday? The fact that she'd barely slept last night probably had something to do with it. At least there hadn't been a tribe of Campbells on her doorstep when she'd returned, for which she was pitifully grateful. She never expected to do the walk of shame at forty-nine years old.

She'd been a virgin when she'd married Waylan at eighteen. And in the years since her divorce, she'd gotten used to going without the intimacies of having a man in her bed. She didn't have casual sex. It simply wasn't how she was wired. Besides, living in a town as tiny as Wishful, the pool of options was small. As a woman, she'd missed the thrill, the comfort of sex. More, she'd missed the companionship—or maybe just the idea of it, as her ex-husband had hardly been a prize in that department. But she'd built a life she loved—one she found fulfilling on its own terms. As mayor, she couldn't afford to have her authority undermined by stepping a toe out of line or giving her constituency anything to speculate about. Public officials were held to a higher standard. Women even more so. Because of that, she'd avoided intimate entanglements rather than have everyone in town discussing who she was sleeping with. As all good Southern women should be, she was a model of propriety and grace. Except, apparently, with Trey.

Her husband.

Opening a cabinet, Adele grabbed a glass and brought the thermos she carried to the table, where Sandy had a death grip on her coffee cup.

"I'm sorry for getting you up so early, but I didn't know what else to do. I can barely function, and I've got meetings this afternoon."

"Never fear. This will cure any hangover." She poured some gray sludge into the glass and nudged it toward Sandy. "Drink up. Just don't ask what's in it."

"Desperate times." Sandy downed it, managing not to choke too much on the vile concoction, before slapping the glass on the table like a shot and gasping.

"Breathe," Adele advised. "It helps. Have you eaten?"

"God no." Her stomach turned over at the thought.

"Then I'm making you some scrambled eggs, while you sit there and tell me exactly what happened after you left Friday night. Spare no details, because I know you didn't come home until Sunday."

"Please tell me that's not common knowledge."

"I haven't heard anybody talking about it. Your car was here. So, spill. Where did Trey take you on your date?"

Sandy curled her hands back around the mug, wishing the warmth made her feel better. "Vegas."

Skillet held aloft, Adele stared. "Are you serious?"

"We took a helicopter from here to the airport in Lawley, where his private jet flew us to Las Vegas. There was a lot of champagne."

"I guess that explains the hangover. What did y'all do there? Gamble? See some shows?"

Sandy hesitated, sipping coffee to buy

more time. She could tell Adele. Adele wouldn't judge. She'd been there. "We got married."

The egg fell from Adele's hand onto the counter and cracked, oozing across the granite. "You did *what?*"

"I should say, we woke up married. Neither of us much remembers the wedding."

"Then how do you know you got married?"

"Well, there were the rings." She'd taken off the wedding band on the flight home—the most awkward three-and-a-half hours of her life, during which she and Trey had both been on the phone, taking care of their respective businesses and all the issues that had arisen in their unplanned absence. But she could still feel the imprint of it on her skin, like a brand.

"Also, the naked." That long, warm, male body all tangled up with hers.

"Vegas is a crazy place. You could've gotten rings without actually getting married."

"Trey tracked down the chapel and confirmed before we left yesterday morning. We got married." Saying it aloud didn't make it feel any more real.

"So, you got married in a wedding you don't remember. What about the wedding night?"

She could still feel the soreness of muscles long unused and that particular loose-limbed sensation of having been well loved. And she couldn't remember a damned thing. Well, okay, that wasn't true. Bits and pieces had come back. Erotic snapshots that made her inner muscles clench. But not the whole. That seemed like the worst part of it all—that her punishment for such a reckless decision was the loss of almost all knowledge of whatever pleasure they'd brought to each other.

"I remember less than I like but enough to know I broke my drought in spectacular fashion."

"Well, congratulations, Mrs. Peyton."

"Don't say that." Sandy shook her head and wished she hadn't. "It was a mistake."

"Are you sure?"

"What do you mean, am I sure? In what

world is a drunk Vegas wedding not a mistake? You, of all people, should remember that."

"Ah, yes, but I married a virtual stranger. You married the guy you've spent thirty years secretly carrying a torch for."

"I have not been carrying a torch for thirty years."

"You haven't let yourself admit it, but you absolutely have. I know you. No matter how drunk you may have been, you'd never have gone through with it unless some part of you actually wanted to do it."

Was that true? Was she blaming the alcohol for a decision she had, on some level, consciously made? Had it made her foolish, or had it simply removed the mountains of inhibitions and doubts so she got out of her own way?

"What did your family say?"

"We certainly haven't told them. The last thing I need is to be judged for yet another hasty marriage. One I put even less thought into than saying 'Yes' to my high school sweetheart." Thirty years of pitying glances and looks over her shoulder to make sure she wasn't screwing up again was quite enough.

"You and Waylan were both young."

"We were. Painfully so. But the young don't have the market cornered on foolish mistakes, as my weekend has made evident."

"What does Trey say about all of this? Does he think it was a mistake?"

This is one of my college fantasies fulfilled... Marrying you.

Sandy had no idea how she should feel about that, though what she did feel was that funny little somersault in her stomach she hadn't felt in years. But she was far too jaded and wary to take that at face value. Oh, she knew he'd cared for her back then. Enough to help her try to escape her marriage. She knew she'd loved him, too. And maybe, in her deepest heart of hearts, she'd dreamed of the kind of relationship with him that she hadn't found with Waylan. But in the intervening years, she'd convinced herself the dream wouldn't have come to fruition. That if she'd left Waylan—with or without Cam being a factor—things with Trey would never have been what she imagined. So little of reality ever matched dreams.

"He thinks he wants this."

Adele frowned. "You say that like he shouldn't."

"He's all caught up in the nostalgia and romance. He's not thinking about the realities of what marriage would mean for us." And God, she'd been there before. Waylan hadn't thought about the realities of marriage either, and look where that had landed them.

The fact was, her reality couldn't live up to the expectations of a man like Trey. She was a small-town girl at heart. A woman with responsibilities to her town. She couldn't go jet setting from place to place, and the necessities of his business would keep him on the move. She wanted—needed—more than that from a marriage. She deserved more. She deserved everything. And for all his assets, she didn't believe Trey could give her that.

"Sandra, you're my best friend, so know that

I say this with the utmost love and sincerity." Adele set the plate of scrambled eggs in front of her. "Get your head out of your ass."

Insult had Sandy snapping her head back. "Excuse me?"

"I know what you've been through. I know your life has been such that you have always been the one in control of everything. The one who had to be responsible, do all the juggling, consider all the practicalities. You've been doing it for so long, you don't even know how to be any other way. But it's time for you to stop being so goddamned practical. Love isn't practical. It isn't perfect. And sometimes it shows up at the most inconvenient times. But if it was easy, it wouldn't be worth it. I think Trey is worth the work of figuring out."

Sandy stared at her. "Who are you, and what have you done with my cynical best friend?"

"I know I'm a cynical bitch, but you have a real shot here. If you don't take it, I'm going to be very disappointed in you."

This was probably not the time to mention

that she'd tried to end things last night and sent Trey on to London. He'd refused to make any kind of a decision while they were both hung over and insisted that they'd discuss it when he got back.

She'd hurt him. She knew that. But he couldn't let his responsibilities slide because of her. No matter what Adele thought, one of them had to be sensible about this. He'd realize that once he got back to his normal life. And when he returned to Wishful for Cam and Norah's wedding, they'd talk about the necessary divorce like the rational, responsible people they were.

So why did the idea of that make her want to weep?

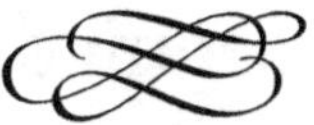

CHAPTER 7

SANDY DROVE HOME IN the wind and rain and decided it matched her mood. She'd almost picked up the phone a half-dozen times today to call Trey. But he was probably in the air or already on the ground in London, and she had no idea what she wanted to say. It felt foolish to just say *I miss you.* Though it was true. How was it that she'd done without him for most of her adult life and after one week of being with him, his absence was a physical ache? She'd have blamed that on the hangover, but Adele's miracle cure had done its job. She no longer had the haze of alcohol or pain to blame her actions on, and regret had settled like the cold, in her bones.

I'm sorry, would certainly be appropriate. But somehow that seemed too small to cover the situation. Why had she pushed so damned hard to send him away? Why not wait, as he'd wanted, and discuss the whole situation when they were both rested and feeling human again? But she hadn't wanted to wait. With the looming specter of Waylan to remind her of all the mistakes she'd made, she hadn't wanted another minute of uncertainty about whether she'd made another. Because she was absolutely terrified of what she felt for Trey. If she gave herself over fully to this relationship, if they tried and it failed, and she lost him again, she didn't think she could survive it. After everything she'd been through—divorce, cancer—it was the broken heart that would do her in.

Sandy was starting to realize it was already too late for that. She was in love with Trey. As

Adele had pointed out, she always had been. She'd just managed to bury it all these years.

Staring into the fire, feeling utterly frozen, she whispered, "Please don't give up on me." He never had, in all these years. But she'd never rejected him quite so utterly.

The pounding on her door made her jolt, sloshing tea over the rim of her mug. Hastily, she set it aside and grabbed a kitchen towel on the way to the door. She didn't want company, but after a weekend without communication, no doubt one of her meddling family was coming to check on her. She was hoping for one of her sisters-in-law. They'd be easier to manage than either of her brothers.

She yanked open the door. "Trey!"

He stood on her front stoop, as if conjured by her longing. His trench coat was soaked and rain streamed down his face, plastering his dark hair to his head. Without hesitation, she reached out and tugged him inside.

"Sorry, I'm dripping on your floor." The innocuous words didn't fit with his serious expression.

She didn't give a damn about the floor. It took everything she had to resist the urge to wrap around him and fix her mouth to his, wet clothes be damned. But after how she'd behaved yesterday, she wasn't sure of her reception. Handing over the kitchen towel in her hand, she said, "I'll get you another towel."

He was *here*, not in London. She'd told him to go, to take care of his business, and he hadn't gone. What did that mean? She didn't dare read too much into it, but her hands shook as she pulled a towel from the bathroom cabinet.

He was still standing there when she came back, though he'd stripped off the coat and hung it on the rack in the corner. "I may have a small lake in my shoes."

"Just leave them by the door. You must be freezing. Come in."

He toed off the shoes and socks, setting them on the little rubber mat intended for that purpose. Taking the towel she offered, he followed her into the living room, mopping off his face and briskly rubbing his head until his hair stood up in boyish spikes. Sandy wanted to reach out and run her fingers through it. She wanted to bury her face in his throat and hang on. But she could sense the tension in him. Lines of strain fanned out around his eyes. She knew she'd been the one to put them there.

Sandy picked up her tea from the side table. "I'm sorry about yesterday." *Oh my God, really? Can you be any more inadequate?*

The corner of Trey's mouth quirked up, but there was no real humor behind it. "I think it's safe to say nobody should be held accountable for anything said under the influence of a hangover."

"Still, I'm sorry I hurt you." She was sorry for so much more than that, but she hardly knew where to begin, and she didn't know what the hell he was doing here.

"I appreciate that." The tone was stiff and formal. Gerald, not Trey.

Sandy gripped her mug like a shield. "I thought you'd be in London by now."

He tossed the towel over a ladder back chair in the corner and met her gaze. "I'm not going to London."

She frowned. "But what about your project?"

"It's being handled by someone else. I delegated. Tess has been jonesing for more responsibility, and she's over the moon to take on a greater role in the company. I spent the entire day delegating because I've spent years surrounding myself with exceptional employees, and it's long past time they had the chance to prove it. My CFO and I have been working to restructure some positions and shift responsibilities so that I can stay here."

They were concessions she hadn't expected from him. More than concessions, they were major changes to his life. And he'd made them for her. He was putting her first. But was he really offering what she thought he was offering? Her heart began to thunder in her chest. "For how long?" She hated that her voice sounded small and afraid.

Trey scooped a hand through his hair in a rare show of restless irritation. "Look, I went about this all wrong."

"About what?"

"This. Us. I didn't do any of this the way I intended. So, let me start over." He carefully took the mug and set it aside, curling his hands around hers.

She felt a tremble and wasn't sure if it was hers or his.

"I love you. I've always loved you. And I know nothing about the situation we find our-selves in is ideal, and I know it's crazy—but I want this. I want you. I didn't fight for you thirty years ago, and it's been the biggest regret of my life. I'm fighting for you now, Sandy. I'll do whatever it takes to make this work. So, I want to know—" He took a step back and sank down to one knee. "—will you stay my wife?"

He'd told her once, back in college, that he'd remake the world for her. Young and scared, she'd thrown that gift away. Now here he was, all these years later, remaking his world, baring everything. The gravity of that left her speechless.

"Trey."

He stared up at her, his Adam's apple bobbing. "I know you're worried about the practicalities, and I—"

Gratitude and relief had her sinking to her knees. "I don't want to be practical. God, I've wasted most of my life being practical."

He was giving her the opportunity for something that could be so much more and he deserved her all.

"Does this mean you'll take a chance? On me? On us?"

All her adult life, Sandy had put others first. Her son. Her family. Her town. For once, she wanted to take something for herself. She wanted to take this chance. Take him. And she wanted to believe it would last. Had to believe it would last.

Giving into the urge to touch him, she

framed his face. "Whatever we have to do, I just want to love you."

His hands came up to cup her shoulders. "To be clear…is that a yes?"

She tightened her arms around him, wanting no room for misinterpretation. "Yes. Yes, I'll stay your wife."

"Then I should give you this." Still serious, he pulled a black velvet box from the pocket of his pants and opened it. The princess cut solitaire was remarkably simple in the elegant, old-fashioned setting. And it suited her far more than some ostentatious display of his wealth.

"Oh Trey, it's perfect. Where did you find time to get a ring?"

"It was my grandmother's. I've been carrying it around since I first came back to Wishful. I told myself I was being foolish, but I couldn't come back to Mississippi without it. Just in case."

Her gaze snapped to his. He'd been carrying this ring for a year and a half? "So long?"

Trey jerked a shoulder and offered a

sheepish smile. "Maybe I buy into the town slogan that this really is the place where hope springs eternal."

She laughed, though a knot of tears clogged her throat.

"It's not the ring I gave my first wife. It wasn't meant for her. I always wanted to give it to you." They both watched as he slipped the ring on her finger. It looked right there, as she felt right in his arms.

Trey lifted her hand to his lips. "I know you probably won't want to wear it in public for a while, at least until we decide to announce it, so I got you a chain. I thought maybe you could wear it as a necklace in the meantime."

Sandy stared. "Did you think of everything?"

"I made a concerted effort. And if you want another wedding somewhere down the line—a proper one, with friends and family, and no Elvis officiating, we'll make it happen."

She winced. "I'm thinking it might be a good thing I don't remember much of that ceremony."

"There's video."

Surely, she hadn't heard him right. "Video?"

"They told me when I stopped by the chapel to ask. I bought a copy, but I haven't been able to bring myself to watch it."

It took a moment to process the stunning horror of that. "I'm not sure how I feel about there being video evidence of our recklessness. If The 'Berg got ahold of that…"

"The 'Berg?"

"As in the tip of the iceberg. It's as close as Wishful has to a tabloid. A few years ago, somebody decided to add a little modern to the gossip mill, so they started a blog. Nobody actually knows who's behind it, and it is, unfortunately, widely read. Video of the mayor's drunk Vegas wedding would be the creme de la creme that beats out Dinner Belles and The Grind. And God knows the internet is forever."

"I don't need the real tabloids getting their hands on it for my own reputation. I'll destroy it."

"Without watching it first?"

"Unless you want to see it, then yeah."

She didn't want to watch it, but it somehow seemed a shame to wipe out the one piece of information that could fill in some of the blanks from their trip to Vegas. "You're not even a little curious?"

"It wasn't the wedding you deserve. None of it was what you deserve. I'll make it up to you."

His expression was so earnest, she couldn't help but reach out to frame his face again. "Okay, let's make a pact."

"About?"

"Let's stop beating ourselves up for how we got married and focus on the fact that we are. I don't want the tone of the rest of our marriage to be tainted with regrets." She stroked her fingers along his nape, staring into his eyes. "I don't regret this, Trey. I don't regret you."

"No?"

Sandy shook her head. "No. In fact, out of all of this, I only have one real regret, other than how I behaved yesterday."

He tensed again. "What's that?"

She ran her hands lightly along the slope of his shoulders before bringing her gaze back to his. "That I don't remember much about what came after the wedding."

The slow smile that spread over his face was full of hot promises and satin sheets. "Well now, I expect we could work on a reenactment of the wedding night."

Heart thumping, Sandy looped her arms around his neck. "That sounds like an excellent plan, Mr. Peyton."

"As you wish, Mrs. Peyton."

Mrs. Peyton. For so many years, she'd been branded by the lingering reminder of her first marriage, opting to keep Crawford for Cam's sake, instead of going back to Campbell. Who knew the prospect of finally being free of it would be so welcome? Or maybe that was the clever mouth Trey had pressed to hers.

Sandy sank into the kiss, into him, letting go of the stress and worry of the past couple of days to just feel.

He laid her back on the thick rug in front of

the fire, his toned body stretching out beside hers. She wanted the weight of him, wanted to peel him out of those wet clothes. She reached between them, fingers fumbling with the buttons of his shirt as he made love to her mouth, seducing her with long, drugging kisses. His hand slipped beneath her shirt and the simple contact was shocking. No one had touched her bare skin in years. Not since…

"Wait."

He nuzzled at her throat. "What's wrong? Uncomfortable? Do you want to move to a bed?"

"Later." She was vain enough to prefer the firelight. "It's just…there are things you probably didn't notice the first time we did this." At the thought of it, the lovely liquid pull in her belly turned to knots.

Trey pressed a kiss to her shoulder. "Neither of us is twenty anymore. You're even more of a knockout now than you were then."

He could make her smile, even now. "You're besotted and have impaired judgment."

Propping himself up on one elbow, he skimmed his gaze over her. "I'm the one doing the looking, so my judgment's the only one that matters in this equation."

The heat in his eyes was beyond gratifying. She clung to that and to him as she said the rest. "I just don't want you to be shocked when you see the scars."

"Scars?" He went very still. "Did Waylan hurt you?"

Recognizing the carefully leashed rage, she cupped his nape, wanting to reassure. "No. No, nothing like that. They're surgical scars." Her fingers trembled faintly as she unbuttoned her shirt, tugging it back to reveal the scar slightly below her collar bone. "This was from my PICC line. For chemotherapy. I had breast cancer."

Voice thick, he murmured her name and lowered his brow to hers. "I could've lost you before I even found you again." He shuddered.

She raked her hand through his hair. "It's okay. I'm three-and-a-half years cancer-free. But I had a double mastectomy and reconstructive surgery. The surgeon did a good job, as far as that kind of thing goes, but I just…wanted to warn you what you were getting into." Some of that was to protect him, but an equal part was a hope that if she warned him, maybe he'd be able to control his reaction, in case he didn't take it well.

Sandy hadn't expected to be nervous. She'd made peace with her post-surgery body ages ago, and she was grateful to be alive and in remission. It was more than so many others ever got. But she hadn't shared that body with anyone until him, and she found his opinion mattered a lot more than she wanted it to.

Trey shifted his hold, cradling her face. "I don't need a warning. I just need you."

God, she hoped that was true.

He stroked a thumb along her lower lip, making it tingle. "Is there anything that hurts? Anywhere that's too sensitive or that I need to otherwise be careful of?"

"No. A lot of the nerves were cut in the

surgery. I've regained some sensation, but I'm not sure how much in this particular context."

"Okay."

He lowered his mouth to hers, unraveling her anxiety with infinite patience and lingering kisses that left her floating. When he parted her shirt, she gave a little hitch. But Trey only kissed her again, smoothing out the edges of her nerves as he smoothed his hands over her skin. Arousal sparked to life, at once new and intimately familiar. Her body, at least, remembered his touch.

She managed, with Trey's help, to get his shirt off, and reared up to press a kiss to his chest, then higher, up his throat. He eased off her shirt the rest of the way, holding her close as he nudged down the strap of her bra. His mouth followed it down the slope of her shoulder, her arm, before repeating the motion on the other side. She felt him pinch and release the catch, and held her breath as he drew it away, leaving her chest bare.

Trey bent his head, pressing a reverent kiss

between her breasts, over her thudding heart. "You're beautiful."

He made her feel beautiful and cherished. Emotion welled up alongside the heat as she accepted the gift of this vibrant, thoughtful man, who'd chosen her, despite everything.

He eased her back again, kissing his way down her torso as he unfastened her jeans and worked them off. His eyes gleamed in the firelight as he took her in from head to toe—scars, stretch marks, and all. "Mine."

The possessive edge to his voice had heat blooming low. Then his hands slipped between her legs to stoke the flames, and she forgot about anything else. He tortured her with ruthless patience, dragging her just to the edge, then shifting rhythm to drive her higher still, until she was gasping his name, begging. He pressed his fingers deeper and she shattered, the orgasm ripping through her like a storm.

Boneless, she lay before the fire, searching for breath.

"I love your legs," he said conversationally. "You've always had glorious legs."

"Oh?" she rasped.

He moved lower and picked one up, pressing a kiss to her ankle. "Miles long. I've spent so much time imagining them wrapped around me." As if to demonstrate he slipped between them, hooking her knees over his shoulders.

"Oh." It came out a squeak as he kissed the tender skin of her inner thighs, his stubble scraping gently, making her tremble. She felt exposed and vulnerable with him down there—and unbearably turned on.

"You'd probably be perfectly scandalized at the things I used to think about doing to you back in college."

Lifting her head so she could look down her body at him, she threaded her hand in his hair. "Let's find out."

Trey smiled, wicked and wonderful. "As you wish."

She wasn't scandalized. She was seduced—

thoroughly and with no mercy, until she forgot everything but his name and the desperate need he built inside her. When he filled her, she wrapped around him, holding tight as they lost themselves to oblivion.

CHAPTER 8

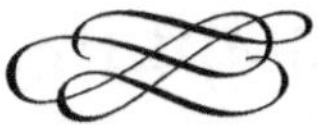

TREY MEANT TO LEAVE at a respectable hour. Really, he did. But somewhere after round two, as he lay curled with Sandy in her bed, filling in the gaps of what they'd done with their lives in the past decades, he convinced himself it would be okay, as long as he left in the wee hours, so the neighbors wouldn't see his car in the morning. Except he'd fallen asleep, wrapped tight around his wife, and somehow dawn was breaking.

"You have to go!" Sandy tried shoving him out of bed.

Trey just tugged her back and rolled her beneath him. "I can think of much better ways to start the morning."

She gave a moan that was half frustration, half arousal before slapping him on the ass and shoving again. "If Delia Watson next door sees your car here, it's going to be all over town by breakfast that you spent the night with the mayor."

"I spent the night with my wife." Saying it still made him grin like ten kinds of idiot.

"Which nobody can know yet. So, you have to go. Before she lets Southern Baptist out to do his morning business."

He couldn't have heard that right. "I'm sorry. Southern Baptist?"

"Her dog. Keep up!"

"You can't not explain that one."

Sandy gave an exasperated sigh. "Delia got into an argument with Odette Simmons from the Presbyterian Church about whether or not pets have souls. Odette insists they don't and therefore don't go to heaven. Delia insists that, of course, her dog will. He's Southern Baptist. They nearly came to blows over it, and Delia makes it a point to walk SB by Odette's yard at least once a week to indicate what he thinks of her by peeing on her hydrangeas. But SB is the least of our worries if Delia sees you. You do *not* want to get on the Casserole Patrol's radar!" She wiggled out from under him and began frantically searching the floor. "Where are your clothes?"

Trey propped himself up in bed and admired the view. "Probably in the living room, as that's where you got me naked."

She went racing out of the room, grabbing a robe on the fly. Clearly, she was serious about this.

With a yawn and a sigh, Trey rolled out of bed. As soon as Norah and Cam's wedding was over, that honeymoon was going to be his top priority. Along with figuring out when and how they could reveal their own marriage because he had a feeling today wouldn't be his last day of sneaking around like a teenager after curfew.

Sandy hustled back into the room and shoved his clothes at him. "Hurry!"

Trey snagged her around the waist and reeled her in. "Hey, slow down. Everything will be fine. We're not doing anything wrong."

"I know, but I don't want people to think—"

To put an end to whatever objection she was about to make, he kissed her. She sighed and wrapped her arms around him, fitting her body to his in a way that had him dropping the clothes and backing toward the bed.

"No. No! We don't have time for this. You have to go! I swear, it won't be forever."

Trey sighed. "Fine. But we definitely have to figure out a better system until we go public with this." He let her go and began to get dressed.

"Trey?"

He lifted his gaze to hers.

"I love you."

Well, damn if that didn't just make everything better.

Fifteen minutes later, he was calling himself

an idiot as he snuck in through the service entrance of his hotel, surprising the housekeeping staff and making up some kind of malarkey about a surprise inspection and keep up the good work. Given his suit was wrinkled and stiff from having dried in a wad on the floor, they probably didn't believe him. He could only hope that the fact that he signed their paychecks would buy him a little discretion. At least they didn't know where he was coming from.

He spent most of his shower split between reliving last night and trying to come up with a better plan. The simple fact of the matter was that after thirty years apart, he didn't want to be away from Sandy. Not for a single night. Achieving that was going to require some even more significant changes to how he ran his business. Probably he shouldn't yet spring it on his CFO that he'd be fully moving to Mississippi in short order. Bruce was still reeling over yesterday's changes. Better to give the guy a little chance to adjust, wait until it was safe to announce he'd gotten married. Everyone would be more cooperative then. He already had the best in telecommuting technology installed here. They could make it work.

Ready to hit the ground running on business, Trey drew up short when he stepped into his office to find Brody. "Good morning. I wasn't expecting you."

His former project manager rose from the chair. "Sorry about that. Louis let me in and said you'd be along shortly." Brody nodded toward the bar. "He made coffee."

Thank God for that. Trey went to pour himself a cup. From the look on Brody's face, he was going to need it. "What's the problem?"

"I just came from the church and a meeting with my night crew foreman. As you know, we had to do some more demolition to get the structure to a place where we could effectively tie in the repairs."

"You found another problem," Trey guessed.

"A mac daddy of a problem. There's massive termite damage. From my analysis, three-quarters of the structure is impacted. It's going to take far more extensive repair, and there's just no way it'll be ready in time for the wedding."

"Well, shit. The wedding is five days away."

Brody spread his hands. "I wish I had better news. I know it took forever for Cam and Norah to set a date around work schedules and town projects. At this point, they may just go down to the courthouse and have done with it."

Trey wanted better than that for Norah. "There's got to be something we can do."

"With all due respect, sir, I don't know that this is a problem you can fix with money and connections."

He heaved a sigh. "Well, I'm not ready to give up just yet. Hang on a minute."

Sandy answered after the first ring. "Miss me already?"

The smile in her voice tugged one of his own. "I do, but that's not why I'm calling. Brody's in my office." Trey glanced up to find his former project manager brows up and knew he'd heard her side of the conversation. Ignoring that, he relayed the problem.

"Damn," she muttered. "Okay, time for plan B."

"There's a plan B?" First he'd heard of it.

"An inkling of one."

"And what might that be?"

"Norah and Cam saved the town. Now it's Wishful's turn to return the favor."

THE DIN of voices filling the community center was enough to make Sandy's head pound, but the noise was worth it to see the turnout of those who'd answered her call for aid in pulling off Cam and Norah's wedding. Her heart swelled at the sheer number of people filling the bleachers and overflowing into standing room at the periphery. God, she loved her town.

She scanned the faces, looking for Trey. He'd been tied up in meetings all day and wasn't sure he'd be able to get loose. Seeing no sign of his dark head, she opted to get the ball rolling. So far, she'd managed to keep this meeting on the relative down low, but her niece, Miranda, would only be able to run interference with the bride and groom for so long. Nodding to Jay Quimby, their city tech guru, she accepted the microphone and took her position at the front of the gym, beneath the basketball goals.

"Thank you all for coming, and so quickly. By now, you're all aware that the Episcopal Church has not only suffered storm damage but that the repair efforts headed up by Jensen Construction have uncovered extensive termite damage. Numerous invitations have been extended around town to see that the congregation is welcome for services, but we're left with the issue of a wedding without a venue, set for this weekend." Sandy strode out toward the center of the gym, meeting the eyes of friends, neighbors, business owners she'd known for years. "My question for all of you is what we're going to do to see that Cam and Norah's wedding still happens on time."

"They can have my barn!" Abe Costello piped up. "It hasn't had animals in it for a good three years, and could be done up right cute with a good cleaning and some twinkle lights." The idea of the cantankerous owner of the Wishful Co-Op and Farm Supply handling twinkle lights was enough to warm Sandy's heart. But he had, after all, made a pretty penny when Norah purchased more than two hundred acres of his family land.

"But is there space for all the guests?" Babette Wofford, owner of Brides and Belles, asked. "How many are y'all expecting?"

"Two hundred at last count," Sandy announced. "Many of whom are coming from out of town."

"What about a backyard ceremony? I've got space for a bunch of folding chairs and a pretty little spot at the edge of the woods," Lorna van Buren offered. "And Cam put in such a sweet garden back there last summer."

Molly Montgomery, co-owner of Wishful Discount Drugs and head of the citizen's coalition Norah founded nearly two years before, stood up. "If you're going outdoor ceremony, why not have it out at Hope Springs in the park? Cam designed it, and Norah donated the land, so it seems fitting."

Sandy felt hope begin to stir. This was the beginnings of a plan. "It's a thought. And certainly, the location is plenty meaningful to them both." They'd fallen in love during the fight to save the land around Hope Springs from GrandGoods, the big box warehouse store that had wanted to set up shop right on its banks.

Cassie Callister, owner of the Daily Grind, clapped her hands with enthusiasm. "We could certainly rent enough chairs, set up an arbor or something with flowers right by the lake. It could be beautiful."

Tyler Edison, Brody's fiancée, spoke up. "There's no power source out there, though.

You'd be working off generators, which would be pretty noisy."

"And what about rain?" Mama Pearl asked. "Ain't nobody know what the weather's gonna do this time of year. Could be gorgeous, could be a monsoon."

"The green." A low, male voice carried above the babble of the crowd.

Searching it out, Sandy pivoted toward the door to find Trey standing, suit jacket draped over one shoulder, shirtsleeves rolled up, and his tie loosened. Everything in her wanted to stride over and bury her hands in his thick hair and kiss him. The image was so strong in her mind, she entirely lost her train of thought. "What?"

"Have it on the town green," he said. "It's a central location, large enough to accommodate chairs and such for an outdoor ceremony, and a sizable event tent for the reception. There'd be power easily available. And it's so...them. That's where Norah started bringing this town back to life."

A murmur swept through the assembly and it occurred to her that most here probably had no idea who Trey was.

Sandy beamed. "That's...perfect. They fell in love over saving the town. What better place to take their vows than in the middle of it?"

He inclined his head in acknowledgment of the point, his own lips curving in a secret smile that had a flush creeping up her neck. Sandy quickly turned away.

"Is that kind of thing allowed in the city?" Molly asked.

"I'm the mayor. And I can't think of a single person who'd object." Sandy shot a glance at the three city councilmen and women in attendance and got no resistance.

Tucker McGee, one of Cam's groomsmen, spoke up. "Not to be a party pooper, but that still doesn't cover the issue of rain."

Trey fielded that one, too. "Tents can be rented. That'd cover rain and wind. And we could get some heaters if it turns cold."

"Would something like that be available on such short notice?" Sandy asked.

"I'll see that they are, if that's what we decide to do."

He'd buy a set himself if they weren't available. She'd learned that much about him. After the meeting, they'd have to have a word about the responsibility of expenses. The church repairs might have been a tax write-off, but the tents wouldn't be, and she didn't feel right allowing him to foot the bill.

Discussion after that turned fast and furious. Molly divided everyone into work groups and Sandy let her. If there was one thing she'd learned to do as mayor, it was how to delegate. And as one of Sandy's oldest friends, Molly would make certain things were done right. By the time everyone filed out forty-five minutes later, there was a plan in place and Sandy actually had faith they'd pull it off. As Mama Pearl had said, everyone loved Cam and Norah and wanted to see them happy.

"Madam Mayor." Trey sidled up as she finally bid Molly good night. "That was quite the turnout."

Behind him, Molly went brows up, pointing at Trey and fanning herself.

Sandy held in a snort of laughter and answered Trey instead. "That is Wishful at its finest."

"It's one of the things I appreciate most about this town. How y'all come together for a good cause. It's the kind of thing you want to be able to say about the place you call home." There was a gravity to his words that made her wonder if he was making more than idle conversation.

"Well now, little sister, when were you planning on introducing us to your…friend?"

Big brothers never ceased to be annoying. Smoothing her expression into unperturbed lines—it wouldn't do to let him know he was getting to her—Sandy turned to face her eldest brother Peter. His wife Liz stood at his side, her eyes jumping between Sandy and Trey with avid curiosity. Bless her nosy, romantic heart. If they managed to keep their marriage under wraps for longer than a few weeks, it would be a miracle.

Undaunted, Trey offered his hand. "Gerald Peyton. My friends call me Trey."

Sandy shot him a look. It was the first time she'd heard him introduce himself as Trey since college. "Trey, my brother Pete and my sister-in-law, Liz."

The men shook, and she didn't miss the subtle power play there.

Oh, for God's sake.

"Appreciate you helping out with the wedding," Pete said.

"Happy to. I'm very fond of Norah."

"You've been spending an awful lot of time with my sister."

"Peter," Sandy barked.

Her brother didn't even blink at the rebuke. "Just looking out for you."

"In case it's escaped your notice, I'm a grown woman, who can look out for herself, and has for several decades now."

"It's nice to see how close all you Campbells are as a family," Trey said easily. "I look forward to getting to know y'all better."

"Well, isn't that just lovely to hear?" Helen purred. "I say bring him to family dinner. Tomorrow night."

Sandy wished for a wall to thunk her head against. "It's Ava's welcome home dinner tomorrow night, Mom."

"Exactly! More reason to celebrate!"

"Ava?" Trey asked.

"My other niece," Sandy explained, her mind already spinning for some kind of excuse. Spending time as a couple with her entire family was entirely out of the question. "Reed's sister. She's a photojournalist, who's spent the past five years in the Middle East. It's rare she makes it home these days, but she wouldn't have missed this wedding for the world."

Trey was smiling like the cat that got the canary. "She sounds like a fascinating young woman. I look forward to meeting her. Thank you for inviting me, Mrs. Campbell."

Her mother blushed. "Oh now, you call me Helen. Seeing as we're getting to know each other and all."

As her family closed ranks, Sandy couldn't help but think, *We are in big trouble.*

CHAPTER 9

FACED WITH THE ENTIRE contingent of Campbells, Trey wondered if he could get them all to list off name, rank, and serial number. It might make them easier to remember. Miranda, the doctor, and Mitch, the architect, belonged to Sandy's eldest brother, Pete, and his wife Liz. Reed, who owned the local bookstore, and his sister Ava, the prodigal Campbell whose return they were celebrating, belonged to middle brother, Jimmy, and his wife Anita. Then there were Cam and Norah, and Reed's fiancée, Cecily Dixon. And

Helen, the matriarch. There was definitely no forgetting Helen. Trey wasn't sure if he should be more scared of potential interrogation or of being lured in by her charm. She had it in spades.

In the wake of dinner—a most excellent pot roast—they'd retreated to the living room. Multiple conversations ping-ponged around the room. He took a seat on the piano bench, content to sit back and watch. As a whole, the Campbells were a messy, involved, obviously loving family. It was such a contrast to the stiff upbringing he'd endured.

"You have a really big family," he murmured as he accepted a post-dinner glass of wine from Sandy.

She hummed agreement as she sat beside him and lifted her own wine. "Nosy, too."

That had been obvious in the less than subtle queries lobbed his way. But between Norah's skillful intervention—God love her—and his own experience with routine press interviews, it hadn't been too bad. And when questions edged too close to the secret they were keeping, it was easy enough to redirect the conversation to Ava and what she'd been covering in Afghanistan or to how the wedding plans were shaping up.

"Just have to make it through dessert, then smooth sailing." Trey was ready to call the night a success.

"Assuming Pete ever gets back with the ice cream. What's taking him so long?"

"I don't know, but if he doesn't hurry, I'm eating his share of apple pie," Cam announced.

"While we're waiting, I just want to take the opportunity to say how much we appreciate your help with our wedding, Gerald," Norah said.

"I'm just one of many, but it's my pleasure. And you'll be happy to know, the tents have been ordered and should be here tomorrow."

"Have Louis send me the bill for the rental," Sandy said.

As if he was actually going to do that. Her salary as a public official was hardly enough to cover such an expense. But Trey understood the mix of pride and independence behind the request, and he'd already sorted out how to get around it. "I decided to buy a set for The Babylon. My events coordinator is delighted to have more to offer future clients, so everybody wins. Who knows? Maybe y'all will start a trend with weddings on the green."

Sandy frowned. Trey looked back, knowing whatever argument she might make had no leg to stand on. Before she could lodge any further protests, the front door opened and Pete came in.

"About time!" Jimmy announced. "We were about to blaspheme and have pie without the a la mode."

"I had good reason for delay."

The easy, teasing mood evaporated at his serious tone. Pete's attention fixed on Sandy. Trey tensed, his body going on alert at the feeling of threat in the air. He automatically wrapped an arm around her, wanting to shield her from whatever was to come. Something flickered over Pete's face at the gesture.

"Whatever it is, spit it out," she said.

"Waylan's back in town."

Trey felt the quick jerk of surprise and the quivering tension that coiled in Sandy's shoulders, and he tightened his grip.

Her head fell forward as she pinched the bridge of her nose. "Of course, he is."

Pete offered Trey an apologetic look. "Sorry to drag you into family drama. Waylan is—"

"I know who he is." Trey couldn't keep the growl from his voice.

Across the room, Norah's gaze sharpened, zeroing in on his arm around Sandy's shoulder, on the hand she'd lifted instinctively to cover his, linking them. Trey gave a short, sharp shake of his head. He'd deal with that later.

"Where?" Cam's one quiet word held a wealth of rage that Trey could respect. He felt an equal measure bubbling in his own blood— thirty years of banked frustration and leashed protective instincts.

"I don't know where he's staying, though the list of options certainly isn't long," Pete continued. "He was sitting at the light when I came out of McSweeny's."

Miranda stood, her hands curling to fists. "Wouldn't take long to find out. A few phone calls, at most."

"Are you sure it was him?" Liz asked.

"Positive."

"Please tell me he's gone bald and acquired a beer belly over the past twenty years," Anita put in.

Pete shook his head, setting the ice cream on the coffee table. "No. He looks almost exactly the same. Older. But still recognizable."

"Your hands aren't bruised, so I know you didn't chase after to confront him." Sandy had gone pale, but her voice was steady.

"Against my better judgment, no," Pete admitted.

Mitch cracked his knuckles. "I say we make those calls, stick dessert on the backburner, and go find a handy rail to run the son of a bitch out of town on."

"I'll drive," Helen declared.

Trey approved of how they immediately circled the wagons. Campbells clearly protected their own. It made him feel a little better, knowing she hadn't been entirely alone in those years after he'd left.

"None of you are doing anything." Sandy rose, giving each of them a long look that said she meant business. Her gaze landed on Trey, those hazel eyes spitting fire. "None of you," she repeated.

Are you fucking kidding me?

She'd done this in college. Forbad him from interfering every time he'd wanted to thrash Waylan for making her cry. Trey hated being hamstrung now as much as he had then. But for her sake, he worked on chaining down his temper.

"I'll handle it," Sandy insisted. "I've always handled it."

Pete snapped to attention. "What do you mean you've always handled it?"

"When did you last hear from him?" Jimmy demanded.

She blew out an irritated breath. "Most recently…about four years ago."

Cam exploded up from his seat. "When you were in the middle of—"

Sandy cut him off, her words simmering with frustration and impatience. "Yes. And I dealt with it."

In the middle of her chemo treatment. The bastard had harassed her, while she was being ravaged by cancer and poison. The temper Trey had tamped down flared with a vengeance.

"You should have told me, Mom. You should have let me handle it. Handle him."

"I know exactly what your version of handling it would entail, and I'm not having you brought up on assault charges against your father."

"It'd be worth it," Cam growled.

"And it would solve nothing."

Quivering with frustration, he stared his mother down. "It's my job to protect you."

"Same goes. You're still my baby." Sandy crossed and took his face in her hands. "He doesn't have the power to hurt me anymore, Campbell. He hasn't for years. He's just an…irritation. An inconvenience. I'll never let him be more than that. Not again."

"Why is he even in town?" Norah asked.

"Maybe he wants to see Cam?" Cecily suggested. She seemed the least blood-thirsty of the group.

"He hasn't bothered with that since I was sixteen." Trey could hear the hurt and resentment beneath the flat, matter-of-fact words and knew exactly why Sandy had chosen to handle Waylan herself.

"Maybe he's here for the wedding?" Liz suggested.

"I don't know how he'd know," Sandy said. "We certainly didn't invite him."

"It's been all over Facebook. He's bound to

still be friends with somebody here," Norah pointed out.

"Why did he come back before?" Trey asked, proud that his tone came out as conversational instead of a roar.

The color was back in Sandy's cheeks, though whether it was from embarrassment or temper, Trey couldn't say. She shrugged. "It's always the same. He wants money because he's blown what he has in pursuit of the next big thing. I never give it, and he slinks back off to whatever hole he came from. He'll do the same this time."

Something didn't feel right about that, apart from the utter wrongness of the fact that he'd come back to the woman he left practically destitute and asked for more. But Trey filed that away to deal with later. "He's easily dealt with."

Her gaze snapped to his. "Don't. I'll handle it."

Trey rose from his seat and prowled over to her. "Like you handled it thirty years ago?"

Temper flared in those hazel eyes and a

muscle jumped in her jaw. "I did what I thought was best."

"You were wrong." This wasn't the time or place for this conversation, but Trey couldn't seem to stop the words. "You were wrong then, and you're wrong now. This pacifistic, path of least disruption isn't the way to deal with a threat, as evidenced by the fact that he keeps coming back."

She rolled her eyes. "He's not a threat. He's an annoyance. You going off half-cocked makes him more important than he is. Just let it go."

Let it go? Was she insane?

"No. You don't get to ask that of me. Not again. Not now." He took a step closer, reaching out to cup her cheek, brushing a thumb over the shadow his memory clearly cast on her face. "Do you think I've forgotten?"

She sighed, a mix of exasperation and disbelief. "It's been thirty years."

And he remembered like it was yesterday. "There is no statute of limitations on an ass kicking for striking a woman."

Everyone started talking at once, shouting in outrage, making demands. Obviously, that was a detail her close-knit family *hadn't* known. Sandy just closed her eyes and turned away from him, stepping away from his touch.

It felt like a slap, another rejection of his protection and his right to look out for her.

A piercing whistle cut through the clamor. Norah. "Let's everybody calm down."

"I will calm down when someone explains what the hell is going on." Pete turned a glare on Trey. "There is clearly more to your relationship with my sister than either of you have let on."

If only you knew.

Trey stayed silent, leaving Sandy to answer.

But it was Norah who fielded the question. "They went to college together." She looked at Trey, apologetic. "I figured it out months ago."

It didn't surprise him. She was an exceptionally smart woman, and there couldn't have been that many married college freshmen from

Wishful at Ole Miss at that time. "Why didn't you say anything?"

She shrugged. "I figured if you wanted to reconnect, you would. Took you long enough."

He wasn't touching that one with a ten-foot pole.

"In the version of the story you told me, you said her husband had never been violent." There was censure in Norah's tone.

"I left quite a few details out of the version you heard." And Sandy had always insisted Waylan *wasn't* violent, despite evidence to the contrary.

"I'm sorry, why am I just now hearing about this?" Cam demanded, staring at his bride.

"It wasn't my story to tell."

"Wait, so you two were…*involved* in college?" Liz asked carefully.

Sandy scooped a hand through her thick blonde hair. "We were friends. That was all."

"Friends," Trey repeated, incredulous. She'd just reduced everything between them to nothing more than friendship. Had all the hours of confidences, the countless shirts she'd soaked with her tears, the unquestioning and unflagging support meant so little?

"I wasn't unfaithful," she said evenly. "Not even when I decided to leave Waylan."

"Because he hit you?" Helen's voice trembled on the question.

"No. Not directly. He was an unmitigated ass when he was a freshman pledge. Drank and partied too much. We fought about it often, and Trey was my confidant."

Trey picked up the thread. "Joseph—Norah's father—was president of his fraternity. So, I went to him to tell him to get his pledge in line. He just said it wasn't his place to interfere in someone's marriage, and told me I'd do well to remember the same."

Sandy's gaze shot to his. "You went to Joseph?"

"Since you forbade me from going after Waylan directly, I had to do something."

"That must be what set him off," she murmured.

"What?" Trey's hands curled into fists, a sick feeling setting up in his gut. Had he been the one who'd indirectly caused the fight where she'd gotten hurt?

"He came home furious, saying he'd gotten in trouble with the fraternity for his behavior. He was just doing what the rest of his pledge class was doing, so why had he been singled out? He was pacing the apartment, ranting whatever his justification of the week was, and I happened to be too close when he turned around. He always used to talk with his hands, and he caught me across the cheek." She folded her arms, defensive. "It was an accident. I know you never believed that, but I swear it's true. He never laid a hand on me again after that one time."

"How about we circle back to the part where you were leaving him," Jimmy suggested. "Clearly that didn't happen. Did he threaten you?"

"No."

"Then why?" Pete demanded. "You know we'd have supported you dumping his ass."

Maybe Trey should've gone to talk to her brothers all those years ago. It seemed like they'd have absolutely been on the same page.

"Because of Cam," Norah said.

Sandy stared at her. "How did you…?"

"Clever girl," Trey murmured.

"You told me you'd planned to get her away after the semester was over. I did the math." She shifted her attention to Sandy. "You'd have been six or eight weeks along by then."

"You stayed in that hell, gave up a chance at another life, because of me?" Cam's voice was dull with shock.

Sandy took Cam by the arms. "Don't you dare blame yourself, Campbell. You are the best thing to ever happen to me, and I have *no regrets.*"

Trey wished he could say the same. But he was too busy remembering every time she'd called him off, talked him down from giving Waylan the beat down he deserved. She hadn't let him stand for her then. Maybe she'd justified it at the time because it had been Waylan's ring on her finger. But it was Trey's she carried now.

"Accident or no, if you think I'm letting him get within fifteen feet of you, you're sadly mistaken."

Sandy whirled on him, and the stubborn set to her chin was so fucking familiar. "It's not your fight. It never was."

"The hell it's not." She was his wife, for God's sake. His to protect. "I should've broken him in half the first time he made you cry."

"I am *not* some naive, defenseless, damsel in distress. When are you *all* going to get it through your heads that I can run my own life?"

"That's not the point!" he thundered. "I want to stand for you. I've always wanted to stand for you, and every goddamned time you pull me back."

"I don't need you to ride in like some knight on a charger to come to my rescue. I don't want that from you."

I don't need you. I don't want you. The blows

landed, a quick one-two punch that pushed Trey over the edge. It was just like college all over again. He shook his head as realization sank into him. This was never going to change. She was never going to change.

He blew out a breath, striving for a calm he didn't feel. "If that's what you think I'm doing, then you don't know me at all. And that tells me everything I need to know."

Needing to escape, he turned toward the door. "You were right when you said this could never work. But not for any of the reasons you thought. It takes two people to make a relationship work, Sandra. And you're clearly not really in this one."

The blood drained from her face. "Trey, I—"

He lifted a hand to ward off whatever excuse she was about to offer. "Just save it. I'll see myself out."

And without another word or a backward glance, he walked away from his wife.

SANDY MADE it to the Mudcat not long before closing. It had taken far too long to wade through the shitstorm Trey had left in his wake. There had been a multitude of reasons she'd never told her family about anything that had happened in college, and every single one of them had played out tonight. Damn Trey. She was exhausted, heartsick, and still furious by the time she strode up to the bar.

Adele took one look at her and groaned. "Aw hell. Joe, take over."

Without a word, Sandy followed her back to the office.

Adele shut the door and crossed her arms. "What happened?"

Too restless to sit, Sandy paced the tiny space. "I am this close to asking you to pull out Bob the Bastard, so I can execute the Three Furies on every man in my life."

Adele lifted a brow. "Somehow I don't think a trio of shots and throwing darts at our resident voodoo doll is going to fix what's ailing you. Tell me what happened."

"Waylan. It's always Waylan. He's like an infection that keeps coming back at the most inopportune times."

"The bastard is bothering you again? Let me close up. I'll get my shotgun."

Sandy blew out an exasperated breath. "You're not helping. I haven't even seen him. But Pete did, and he came over to Mom's tonight, where the entire family and Trey were waiting on dessert." Sandy filled her in. "The lot of them were like a lynch mob."

"Point me to the nearest pitch fork."

"What *is* it with everyone who knows me wanting to string him up by the balls?"

Adele gave her a flat stare. "Um, because he hurt you, left you near to destitute, and it's no less than he deserves?"

"But don't any of you understand? He's not *worth* the upset. He is not worth making a fuss or a scene over. Because it plays into his ego. It makes him feel important, like he's still relevant to my life, when he's *not.* Apathy is my greatest weapon against him." It had bought her four years last time. Maybe this time it would buy her more.

"You'll have to forgive the rest of us for not being as evolved as you. What did Trey say to all of this?"

"He's just as angry now as he was in college." And how could that be? How could those emotions have continued to fester after all this time? "He pulled this whole He-Man routine that's completely ridiculous." She looked to her friend for support but found disapproval instead.

"Put yourself in his shoes, Sandy. A girl you like, one you come to love, uses you as a confidant, talks about her shitty marriage, gets hit by the asshole—accident or not. A real man—a man of integrity and principles—doesn't stand aside and just let it happen."

"Oh, please."

"I'm serious. This is one of those Mars-Venus things. Women can just gripe about things and listen. We get the importance of venting and understand that the telling of problems does not mean we're expected to fix them. But men aren't like that. Men hear a problem and they try to do something about it."

Sandy speared both hands into her hair and tugged in frustration. "There's nothing to *fix*. Waylan is no threat."

"He's a man who was, at the very least, emotionally abusive to you. A man you continually protected at the expense of yourself, when a ready defender was at hand. And now you've married that defender and have told him he doesn't have the right to be that to you. I don't blame Trey for being pissed. It's a fucking slap in his face."

"That's not what I said!"

"Subtext, sugar. I guarantee that's what he heard."

Before she could reply, a knock came on the office door. Adele tugged it open to reveal Pete.

"Thought you might be here." Without waiting for an invitation, he stepped inside. "Give us a few minutes, Adele?"

"Take all the time you want. I need to start close up." She left, shutting the door behind her.

Sandy scowled at her brother. "I don't want to talk to you."

"That's fine. You don't have to talk. But you do have to listen."

"To what, Pete? More reminders about how I should have dumped Waylan sooner? How I should have let the family help? Or how I should have left him even though I was pregnant? Forgive me if I'm sick of having my life choices thrown back in my face as the wrong ones."

He went brows up. "Is that really what you think we're saying?"

"All I have ever felt from y'all on the subject is your disapproval for how I handled things."

He had the grace to look chagrined. "That wasn't our intention. Ever. We just…want him to pay more than he has."

"Your way wouldn't make him pay. It wouldn't bring any kind of restitution or remorse. It would just make things worse for me.

I've endured enough gossip because of Waylan. I have paid for the mistakes of that marriage a hundred times over, and going after him the way y'all want to do is just going to create a spectacle that will drag it all back to light again. I'm *tired* of it." The embarrassment of being in the public eye for scandal again was worse than almost anything she'd endured being married to Waylan.

"We just want to protect you."

"You all keep saying that, like it makes everything okay." Didn't they understand how much of an insult it was? "I don't need protecting. I protected myself and my son perfectly well for years. In case you all missed the memo, I am a strong, independent woman, who was a successful single mother, a respected public school administrator, and who now runs an entire damned town."

"We're not questioning your capabilities."

"Aren't you? The fact is, your desire to attack Waylan isn't about me."

"And what is it about?"

"Your own guilt for the fact that you weren't there. You didn't see and didn't act when you think you should have. You're my big brother. You look at what I went through and think you should've done something."

Pete's hands curled into fists. "Okay. I'll admit there's truth to that. It kills me that I can't go back in time and change what happened. But it's only because I love you, and I hate what that bastard did to you."

"Well, so do I. But Jesus, Pete, if this was really about me, you'd let it go, like I have. Because that's what I want. That's what I need."

Her brother fell silent, clearly weighing his words. "All right. I'll do my best. And I'll talk to the others about the same."

Sandy blew out a long breath. "Thank you."

"The rest of us aren't as even-tempered as you. You're always the calm lake." He turned to her. "Except for tonight. Except with this Peyton guy."

"Your point?"

"We Campbells only really lose our tempers over those we care about."

Unbearably weary, she dropped onto the loveseat. "What do you want me to say?"

"Do you love him?"

"I loved him enough thirty years ago that I was going to walk away from my husband."

"And now?"

She thought of the resignation in his eyes as he'd turned away from her and walked out and felt fresh cracks open in her heart. "After tonight, I'm not sure that it matters."

"He wants to stand for you. Why don't you give him a chance?"

"Because I don't want someone to stand for me, Pete. I want someone to stand *with* me. And I don't know if he's capable of doing that."

CHAPTER 10

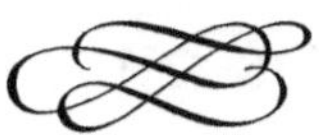

SANDY DIDN'T COME TO him. Trey didn't realize how much he'd expected her to show up and talk through things until the night went by and she didn't darken his door. He was still at his desk, looking out at the green as the sky began to lighten with dawn.

What did that mean? Was she still angry? Had they just retreated to their corners? Or were they really through?

He hadn't wanted to listen. Not with her entire family looking on. Having an audience while she explained why he wasn't worthy was more than he could endure. But he'd really believed she would come to him, if only to try and dissolve things completely. Maybe it was good that she hadn't. In his hurt and anger, he might have let her.

Trey was still furious. She'd said she wanted more than a part-time relationship. Well, he wanted a marriage that was more than name only. He wanted her to trust him, to rely on him. He wanted her to need him. Maybe he'd been kidding himself that they ever stood a shot. She hadn't been willing to share the load at nineteen, and she was no more prepared to do so now. Really, he was a fool to have expected otherwise.

Sandra Campbell Crawford didn't need him. She didn't need anybody. The question was, did he love her enough to live with that?

She deserved everything. She said she wanted everything, but she didn't. Or maybe she didn't know what everything really was.

It wasn't a decision he'd be making until

he'd calmed down and had time to think, to sleep. As neither of those things would be happening any time soon, he spent some time catching up on details of the London project, answering email from Tess, who'd hit the ground running and taken the reins as if she'd been born to them. He supposed she had been. She was his daughter, after all. The precious baby girl he'd never have had if Sandy was anyone other than who she was.

But it wasn't the past he was still angry about. It was the now. Checking the time, he shifted focus for the meeting he'd arranged last night.

Waylan wasn't staying at The Babylon. Trey hadn't really expected he would be. If money were truly his motive, the boutique hotel was hardly the budget-friendly option. But he wasn't registered at the Mockingbird Motel, either. Trey had checked as soon as he left Helen's house. That left the B & B or somewhere else. Before the end of the day, he'd know a helluva lot more than where the bastard was staying.

He just wasn't certain what he'd do with the information.

The intercom buzzed. "Mr. Kane to see you, sir."

"Send him in." Trey rose and circled his desk as the office door opened.

A barrel-chested man with a curiously silent walk strode past Louis, a to-go cup of coffee from The Daily Grind in his hand. If Louis had any opinion about the fact that Trey had called the former spook in, he kept it to himself and shut the door.

Kane crossed over and offered his hand. "Mr. Peyton. A pleasure, as always."

"Thank you for coming so quickly."

The man had been out of the country when Trey called the night before. He had no idea which country and hadn't asked. Those were the sorts of details Kane chose not to share and Trey knew better than to ask.

Kane settled into a chair. "What can I do for you, sir?"

Trey hesitated. He was crossing a line here

—one he'd deliberately avoided for three decades. Sandy wouldn't thank him for his interference. But deep in his gut, he knew something was wrong with the entire situation with Waylan. Protecting her was the most important thing, whether she appreciated it or not.

"Standard NDAs apply?"

Kane inclined his head. "Of course. Who's the target?"

"Waylan Crawford. White male, forty-nine, about six feet tall. Formerly married to one Sandra Campbell Crawford, current mayor of Wishful. They divorced about eighteen years ago. I can provide you with a very, very old address. I don't know where he's based now, but as of last night, he was here in Wishful."

"Anything in particular you want to know?"

"Everything. Financials, known associates, job history. I want to know everything this son of a bitch has been up to for the past thirty years."

Kane lifted a brow, the equivalent to a shock

on his usually impassive face. "Thirty years, sir?"

"We go back a long way."

The other man studied him with the kind of flat, assessing stare Trey felt certain he'd used in interrogation. "This isn't your usual kind of request."

"No. It's personal. I believe he's a threat to my wife." No reason to keep that a secret. Kane could ferret the information out in less than five minutes, if he'd a mind to.

"I didn't realize you'd remarried. Congratulations, sir."

"Thank you. It's recent and we haven't announced it yet."

"And would your blushing bride happen to be the former Mrs. Crawford?"

Trey had reason to know Kane's observational skills rivaled those of Sherlock Holmes, but it probably didn't take a former spy to suss that out from the current situation. "Yes."

The silence stretched out as they stared at each other.

At last, Kane nodded. "Okay. Might take some time to dig back that far."

"His current location and reason for being here is priority. He's up to something, and I want to know what. By Saturday morning. Her son is getting married, and I want to be certain Crawford doesn't crash the wedding."

"I'll do my best, sir."

Trey scribbled down Sandy's old address on Maple Street and handed the paper over. "Per usual, discretion is paramount. My wife isn't aware I'm looking into this."

"Understood." Kane rose and prowled toward the door as silently as he'd entered. "I'll be in touch."

JOSEPH BURKE HADN'T CHANGED a whit since college. He was still as long-winded as ever—if eloquent. But he failed to display his daughter's sensitivity to audience as he continued to wax poetic in his toast to the bride and groom.

Sandy resisted the urge to check her watch to see how long he'd been going and instead slowly turned her wine glass by the stem. Thank God, they'd saved toasts until after the main course was served.

At least he wasn't being critical. Poor Norah had been on edge since the moment he'd gotten off the plane. She sat at the center of one of the long tables set up for the rehearsal dinner, hand clasped with Cam's, her face set in stiff, polite lines, clearly waiting for the other shoe to drop.

As waitstaff silently cleared away the dinner plates and began to serve dessert, Sandy saw Norah's mother, Margaret, reach up to tap her ex-husband on the arm, making a clear *wrap it up* gesture.

"In short, I wish you both all the happiness in the world. Cheers." Joseph raised his glass.

Short, my ass. But Sandy raised her glass and murmured "Cheers," along with everyone else before sipping and shoving back her chair. Hers was the last toast.

She skimmed her gaze over the assembled

group, smiling at the groomsmen she'd known since they were boys and the bridesmaids who'd become as close as sisters to Norah, nodding to her brothers, their wives, her mother, before settling on her son and his bride. Trey wasn't among them. He'd sent his regrets for the dinner and the wedding via Louis, saying he didn't want to make anyone uncomfortable or take attention off the happy couple. They hadn't spoken in two days, not since the fight at her mother's. She'd wanted him here beside her to share in the joy of this wedding. His absence had a presence, an invisible weight that left her keenly aware of what she was missing. She felt awful. Yes, he was angry with her, but he'd never have missed Norah's wedding just because of that. He was making the sacrifice for her comfort, to eliminate any awkwardness and keep the focus on Norah and Cam.

Cam's brows drew together in concern, and Sandy realized she'd been standing there saying nothing for far too long. She pasted on a smile. "I'll keep this brief because I know we all want to get to our dessert. Norah, I told you once, when you first got involved with my son, that it's a smart thing for a mother to learn to care for the woman her son chooses, and it's a real gift to legitimately like and respect her. But I had no idea how much I'd grow to love you. You have brought immeasurable joy to Cam's life and to mine, and I couldn't be more delighted to be making you a formal part of the family. Welcome." She raised her glass. "To Cam and Norah."

The sentiment was echoed around the room.

Sandy drank and sat.

Liz leaned close and whispered, "You okay?"

"Fine." She amped up the smile, knowing it was a little strained around the edges. "Weddings just make me emotional. I'm so happy for them."

Her sister-in-law put an arm around her shoulder and squeezed. Sandy knew Liz didn't believe her, but she'd let it slide.

The remainder of the dinner passed in a

blur. The kids kept conversation lively and the general mood was jubilant that the wedding was finally happening, despite scheduling conflicts and storm damage. When the party broke up, they wandered en masse out to the parking lot, exchanging hugs and farewells. Sandy couldn't wait to get home and get out of this suit and these heels. More, she wanted away from the prying eyes of her family. Maybe Trey would be ready to talk.

Reflexively, she dug into her purse for her phone, to check whether he'd called. "Oh, I left my phone inside."

Jimmy and Anita paused by their car. "We'll wait for you."

Sandy waved them off. "No need. Go home. Tomorrow's going to be a long day and we all need some rest."

"Are you sure?" Anita asked.

"Positive. Go."

"We'll see you in the morning," Jimmy promised.

Inside Tosca, Sandy retrieved her phone

from the private room in the back. Trey hadn't called. Biting back her disappointment, she detoured through the bar, for a quick trip to the restroom before heading home. Of course, that meant she got snagged by three different acquaintances and forced to make polite conversation about the upcoming wedding. By the time she emerged from the bathroom, her nerves were shot and her politician's mask was in pieces. She needed to get home.

"Hello, Sandy."

Her heart jolted and she stumbled to a stop as a tall figure peeled off the wall in the short hallway. Irritation replaced the instinctive fear. "What the hell are you doing here?"

Her ex-husband smiled the broad grin she'd once found charming. "Saw you were here and wanted to say hello."

"Goodbye." Sandy shoved by him, striding with purpose toward the door.

Waylan followed. Fine. She'd rather say what she had to say to him in the parking lot. Automatically, she scanned the cars, looking for witnesses. It wouldn't do for her constituency to see her lose her veritable shit with her ex. Seeing no one, she rounded on him. "I don't know what you think you're up to, Waylan, but I told you four years ago, and every other time before that—you will not get another penny from me. So, drag yourself back to whatever rock you crawled out from."

He pressed a hand to his heart. "You wound me, sweetheart."

"Don't you sweetheart me. Just get the hell out of my town."

"It may shock you to hear, I'm not here for money or for you."

That left only one thing. "Cam doesn't want you at the wedding."

Surprise cracked his charmer facade. "Cam's getting married?"

Sandy cursed herself for letting that spill. But if he wasn't here for the wedding or for money from her, then why *was* he here? "That's none of your business."

"He's my son. That makes him my business."

"He stopped being your business when you abandoned him. You were no kind of father to him. You had nothing to do with the raising of him and did everything in your power to avoid a relationship with him. So, no, Waylan, he's not your business. Nothing about his life is your business, and I'm telling you, you can't be here."

"It's a free country, Sandy. I have a right to see my son get married."

The blood drained from her face. Dear God, if he showed up, the wedding would turn into a riot. "Don't do this. If you love him at all, don't ruin his wedding day by crashing it."

"I'm not going to ruin anything. I just want to see him get hitched and wish him well. Where's this whole shindig going down?"

Unbelievable. Abruptly, she thought of Trey. He'd removed himself from the entire event he'd helped orchestrate and largely funded just because he didn't want to make anyone uncomfortable. And here was Waylan, who gave not a damn about how Cam or anyone else felt. Per usual, all he cared about was himself.

"You won't be hearing it from me."

"Doesn't matter. It's a small town. Someone else will tell me."

Sandy wasn't going to continue this conversation. She needed to get out of here before she did something radical, like planting her fist in his face. Apparently, her family's aggression had bled over. Digging out her keys, she unlocked the driver's side door and opened it. Before she could slide inside, Waylan reached out and shoved it closed again.

For the first time, a trickle of unease bled through her temper. "What are you doing?"

"We're not done with our conversation."

"We most certainly are." She yanked on the door handle, but he didn't move out of the way. For the first time in years, she registered her ex-husband as more than an irritation.

A few spaces away, a car door opened and a hulking man slid out. "You okay, ma'am?"

Sandy chanced a glance in his direction. She

didn't know him. By his neutral accent, he certainly wasn't from around here. How long had this guy been sitting there? *Why* had he just been sitting in his car? It didn't matter. He had her gratitude because as soon as he took a few steps toward them, Waylan eased back, lifting his hands in the universal gesture of *no threat,* a smile of apology creasing his cheeks.

Sandy called herself a fool for giving in to Trey's paranoia. Of course, Waylan was no threat. She yanked open her car door. "I'm fine, thank you."

The stranger nodded, his eyes staying on Waylan.

Sandy slipped into the car.

"I'll see you at the wedding," Waylan called.

"I'll see you in Hell," she answered, and slammed the car door.

CHAPTER 11

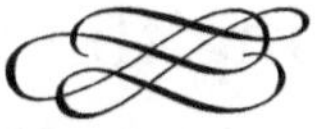

TREY WANTED TO ESCAPE. The town he loved felt like a prison without the woman it represented. He knew a single phone call would have his chopper ready to go. In an hour, he could be leaving the tarmac of the Lawley airport on his jet, headed back to Denver or to London or any number of his other ventures. He had business all over the world, projects that could and probably should demand his attention. He could get back to real life and away from this dream that had turned into a nightmare.

But throwing himself into his work to avoid his marriage was something he'd done before. He couldn't leave without talking to Sandy. They had to resolve things, one way or the other. He had a feeling the resolution would be dissolution—whether he liked it or not. Because as much as he wanted to give her the world, it was not in his power to be the guy who stood aside. That wasn't who he was and wasn't someone he was willing to become. Not even for her.

Neither of them were likely to come out of that conversation unscathed, so it would have to wait. Trey didn't want to do anything else to upset her or otherwise ruin Norah and Cam's wedding. They all deserved better than that.

Preparations were proceeding apace down on the town green. He watched the bustle of people going to and fro. The tents were already put up for the reception and a small army was attaching bows and greenery to the rows and rows of folding chairs lining the sidewalk up to the fountain. The day had dawned sunny and promised to be a balmy sixty degrees—perfect for an outdoor ceremony. His hotel manager had been informed this morning that local law enforcement would be blocking off the roads around the green for the ceremony. One of the perks of the groom's mother being mayor, he supposed. With all the people pitching in to make this happen, the guest list had swelled to encompass most of the town, so they'd need all the space they could get.

He wished he were still on it, but he'd have to settle for watching the proceedings from here in his office.

The intercom buzzed. "Mr. Kane to see you, sir."

At last, answers. "Send him in."

Trey turned from the window to greet the private investigator. "What have you got for me?"

Kane looked calm as ever and Trey had the absurd thought that he never wanted to meet the guy across a poker table.

"Our Mr. Crawford has been a naughty

boy." He pulled a thick folio out of his messenger bag. "I didn't quite make it back thirty years yet, but the past decade should certainly make for interesting reading."

"Highlights?"

Kane dropped into a chair. "He's a guy always out to make a quick buck, and he doesn't seem to care much off who. For years he's toed the line, staying just this side of legal, engaging in smarmy business practices but nothing outright criminal."

So far, nothing Trey hadn't expected.

"Crawford has moved around a lot. Big cities, mostly. He's a smooth talker and has associates that range from stock brokers to grifters. Where he falls on that spectrum is unclear, but the man can't seem to hold on to money. He's got expensive tastes. As soon as he gets his hands on any cash, he's spending it on high end liquor, clothes, lodging. There was a brief flirtation with gambling a little over four years ago, but after losing his shirt—literally, according to the security footage I saw—he's stayed away from that."

"Relationships?"

"Shallow at best. His parents are dead, and he is, as I assume you know, not involved with his son. He's had no serious relationship with a woman since his divorce, and he occasionally touches base with his ex-wife. Including last night."

Trey snapped to attention. "Excuse me?"

"He cornered her in the parking lot at Tosca, after the rehearsal dinner. She was clearly annoyed by him, trying to convince him not to crash the wedding. The wedding he had no idea was going on until she mentioned it. They argued and Crawford got into her personal space."

Trey's hands fisted, aware of the question Kane wasn't asking. Why hadn't he been with his wife? He'd considered trying to mend fences in the name of the wedding. But knowing the steps he'd taken by hiring Kane and that Joseph Burke would be there, he'd decided it would be all around easier on everyone if he gave his regrets and kept himself out of it. But he hadn't truly thought Waylan would show up.

When he didn't fill the silence, the PI continued. "I intervened before the situation could escalate. She was perfectly safe."

The band around his chest loosened a fraction. "What about Crawford?"

"I hung around and trailed him back to his lodgings. An apartment on the east side of town. Looks like an AirBnB rental."

Convenience, Trey wondered, *or an attempt to stay off-grid?*

"Any idea what he's really doing here?"

Kane leaned toward the folio and opened it. "My guess is running from this."

Trey read the document. *Baltimore Police Department. Known associates. Racketeering. Wanted for questioning.*

"It seems he's gotten involved with the wrong people," Kane said mildly. "The FBI has a file on him, BPD is pretty eager to talk to him, and I wager the people they want to talk to him about are just as eager to keep him quiet."

Trey had suspected…something. But ties to organized crime hadn't been it. What kind of danger had Waylan brought with him? "Is there any evidence anyone has tracked him here?"

"Unclear. It took a fair amount of digging for me to unearth his tracks, and it's unlikely either BPD or the Scafidi family has my particular skillset in that department. But he has not, historically, been the sharpest knife in the drawer. If he hasn't slipped up yet, he will."

Trey turned back to the window, looking down at the green and all the people. "Where is he now?"

"He left his car—a rental—parked down past the Baptist Church and was, last I saw, headed into the diner, presumably to acquire information on the location of the wedding, since your wife refused to tell him. Not that it's hard to guess given the setup going on down there. The whole thing is a tactical nightmare. No way to secure the area, certainly not without alarming the populace. And neither of us has the authority to do that anyway."

No. His money could buy all sorts of things, but full control of the town wasn't one of them. "In your professional opinion, do you think there's a legitimate threat?"

Kane didn't hesitate. "Unlikely. But if Wishful PD were to pick up and detain Crawford until the FBI agents I tipped off last night could get here from Baltimore, I imagine that would earn them considerable goodwill." He flashed a rare smile. "I still have a few friends."

Was this really so simple? And was it the right thing? Waylan had made his metaphoric bed. Was it so wrong to make certain he had to lie in it? This certainly seemed the easiest solution to ensuring he couldn't crash the wedding.

Trey picked up the phone and dialed. "I'd like to speak with Chief Greer, please."

"GOD, YOU LOOK SO HANDSOME." Sandy pinned the red rose boutonniere on Cam's lapel and just looked at him—her sweet, steady son—tears pricking her eyes. He'd grown into such a good man.

Never one to miss the subtleties, he cupped his hands beneath her elbows and frowned. "Mom?"

She sniffed. "Don't mind me. I'm just having a moment. You were six years old yesterday, and now you're about to walk down the aisle to marry a wonderful woman and start your life together. I'm a little emotional." She brushed imaginary lint off his tux jacket shoulders.

Cam looked to his groomsmen. "Can y'all give us a few minutes?"

"Sure thing," Tucker said. He and Brody headed for the door.

Mitch paused, slapping a hand on Cam's back. "You've got five minutes before you need to head down to the fountain, cuz. Make it quick. If you're late, I just might marry Norah myself."

Cam grinned. "Keep dreaming."

"Every day, cuz. Every day."

The door shut quietly behind Mitch, and Cam's attention shifted back to Sandy, the grin fading. "I'm worried about you."

She was worried about his father. Through all the preparations today, she'd kept an eye out for Waylan, but so far there'd been no sign. She wanted desperately for this wedding to go off without a hitch, so that Cam and Norah's memory of the day wouldn't be tainted with spectacle and disaster. Which meant she said nothing of her confrontation with Waylan at Tosca last night.

"I'm fine, baby. Truly."

He gave her a look like he knew damned well that was a lie. "You know, I just want one thing as a wedding present."

"If it's in my power, I'll give it."

"I want you to be happy."

"I am happy." What else could she be on the day of her son's wedding?

"Mom." The single syllable stopped whatever argument she would've made.

Clearly, she needed to work on her acting skills.

"You've spent your entire life doing everything for me. And I'm grateful. So damned grateful, because nobody could've had a better mom. But I'm getting married today. And it's long past time for it to be your turn to find what I've got with Norah."

His words re-opened the wound to her heart that hadn't stopped bleeding for days. She'd thought she'd found it. She'd thought life had miraculously brought her full circle, back to the man she'd always loved. But she didn't know how to be the kind of woman who let someone else fight her battles.

"Talk to Trey."

She certainly didn't want to talk about this with Cam. "That's complicated, baby."

"Not really." Cam slid his hands down to link with both of hers. "Do you know what I've learned loving a strong woman?"

Seriously? Her generally quiet son was going to pontificate about love? "What's that?"

"That sometimes I have to step aside and let her do her thing."

Yes. That was exactly what she wanted. Was it so hard to understand?

"But, you know what she's had to learn in return?"

"What?"

"That sometimes I have to step in to protect and defend. Partnership doesn't mean she's weak or incapable. It just means I've got her back. It's been too damned long since somebody had your back, Mom. Whatever stubborn principles you're holding on to...they aren't worth walking away from that."

Well. Sandy had no idea how to respond. So, she said nothing, just nodded and swallowed back the knot of tears in her throat as Cam wrapped his arms around her in a hug.

"Looks like it's time," he said.

They headed down the stairs of City Hall arm-in-arm and crossed the town green toward the fountain. Music played over a PA system, the cheerful strings echoing faintly off the downtown buildings. Guests filled nearly every seat but the front row of chairs, and more were gathered behind and around the seating area. Sandy scanned each face, smiling and nodding to those she knew, but remaining on alert for the one face she didn't want to see. With a quick kiss on her cheek, Cam dropped her off with the gathering of the rest of the family at the back of the crowd and headed for the fountain, where Reverend Prescott waited.

A disturbance drew her attention to the reception tent. With a sinking sensation, Sandy hurried in that direction. Had Waylan tried hiding in there?

But it wasn't her ex-husband she found. It was Norah, arguing with her bridesmaids.

Miranda stood, hands on hips. "Hold her down, Tyler."

"Don't you even." Norah brandished her bouquet like a weapon.

"Then hand it over," Miranda insisted.

Sandy let the tent flap fall and rushed forward. "What's going on?"

"Norah won't give up her headset," Piper said.

Ever the control freak, Norah backed away from her friends, one hand protectively over her ear. "I just want to—"

"Norah, I love you, but you're not walking down the aisle with the headset. Hand it over." Miranda held her hand out, palm up.

"But—"

"Let it go, sugar," Tyler ordered.

Looking a bit mulish, Norah pulled out her earpiece and dropped it into Miranda's hand.

"Good girl."

With an indulgent smile, Sandy took her hands. "I promise everything is taken care of. Molly has it under control."

"I know, I just—"

"You just need to take a deep breath. You're getting married in a few minutes."

Norah's hands trembled. "I keep expecting something else to go wrong."

"There's nothing left to go wrong. The whole town has made sure of it." And if Waylan showed up and made an ass of himself, she'd just have to finally give in and kill him. Nothing was going to ruin their day. "All you have to do is walk down that aisle. Cam's waiting right there by the fountain."

Norah blew out a breath. "Okay."

Voice brisk, Sandy went down the checklist. "You've got your something old."

"My mother's veil."

"Something new?"

"I figured the whole dress counted." Norah's eyes went wide. "Does the dress not count?"

"The dress totally counts," Sandy assured her. "I can see the something borrowed."

She reached toward the pearls at her throat—Sandy's pearls—and smiled. "Yes. Thank you."

"And Cam has you covered for your something blue with the sapphires in your engagement ring."

"He's got me covered for everything." She

said it with an absolute faith that warmed Sandy's heart.

Nodding, Sandy stepped back. "Then I'd say you're ready."

"Oh my God, so ready. Let's do this."

Sandy took her place just as her mother was being seated, her own nerves making her glad she'd remembered waterproof mascara. As the music shifted, Mitch offered his arm, escorting her to her proper place on the front row. It was really happening. Thanks to all the hard work of her town, her boy was finally getting to marry the love of his life. Sandy dug for the tissue she'd stuffed up the sleeve of her suit and cast one more look around for Waylan. Seeing no sign of him, she began to relax a fraction. Maybe this would go off without a problem after all.

Then she saw Trey. He wasn't seated on the bride's side. But he stood just to the side of the far aisle, at the front of the onlookers. And his gaze was fixed on her.

He came. The flood of relief was staggering,

and on its heels came a yearning to touch him that was so strong, she nearly rose from her seat. She'd been on her own for such a long time—raising her son, running her town—she was good at it. It had never occurred to her that she'd want him by her side today, that she'd feel this need to share this special day with him. Only the next change in music, heralding the procession of attendants, kept her in place.

They marched in, two-by-two. Mitch and Miranda. Tyler and Brody. Tucker and Piper. Then came the very unconventional ring bearer. Cam's dog, Hush, pranced—without an escort—down the aisle with more pomp and attitude than should've been possible for a hundred-pound ball of white fluff. The Great Pyrenees-Malamute mix carried a specially-made pillow mounted to her collar. Miraculously, she made it all the way to Cam without stopping to greet all and sundry. As the dog plopped her butt down beside Cam and sat at attention, Sandy let out a breath. As long as there were no squirrels, they'd be safe.

The bridal march began. Those seated stood, and everyone turned to watch as Norah walked down the aisle. From her position up front, Sandy couldn't see her, so she watched Cam instead. The absolute joy on his face warmed her down to the bone. Had she looked like that when she married Waylan? She'd thought herself in love, been happy and excited. But that kind of effervescence in the blood… she didn't remember that.

Had she had it when she married Trey?

Instinct had her searching for his face, wanting to connect and share this moment with him. Her eyes met his and everything melted away but him. The generous, loving man who wanted to have her back. Could she let her guard down and trust him enough to do that?

Norah passed to the front of the crowd, pulling Sandy's attention back to the ceremony. She was radiant as she glided up to the fountain and placed her hand in Cam's.

"Dearly beloved and citizens of Wishful—"

The assembled crowd chuckled. "We are gathered here today to celebrate the union of Norah and Campbell."

Sandy cried. Quietly and with as much dignity as she could muster. But her baby was getting married. She figured she was allowed.

"They'd like to say a few words to each other." Reverend Prescott held out a hand to indicate they could begin.

Norah turned to hand off her bouquet to Miranda, and Cam took her hands, raising them to his lips to gently kiss her knuckles.

"I know you've memorized yours, but I hope you don't mind that I jotted down a few bullet points." Reaching into his breast pocket, he pulled out an index card. "Norah Burke, the moment I laid eyes on you, the first thought that went through my mind was, 'Wow!' I don't think I've ever told you that. Not a day has passed that you haven't made me think 'Wow!' You do so much and care so much about me, about our families, about this town—it's amazing. *You* are amazing."

He glanced down at the card and tossed it so he could cup her cheek. "Wishful sees General Burke or Wonder Woman or whatever remarkable persona you're wearing that day and thinks, 'That woman never stops. She's always doing her duty to everyone.' But they, and even you, don't know that duty isn't what drives you. It's love. You have so much love inside you that you have to have a place to put it, and I thank God every night you chose me and this town. You made me a promise that you'd save my world. I had no idea you'd actually become my world in the process. You're the strongest person I've ever known. You're stubborn, dedicated, and you don't give up—ever. I can't imagine better qualities in the woman I want by my side for the rest of my life."

Cam grinned, his dimples flashing. "I think I missed a couple of bullet points. I hope that's okay."

Tears streamed down Norah's cheeks. "It's totally okay. Just be glad I had waterproof mascara on one of my lists. Cam," she began, swiping at her cheeks and squaring her shoulders. "I used to be a dedicated workaholic." Cam arched a brow and Norah laughed. "Okay I'm still a dedicated workaholic. I didn't think I was made for love. I had a purpose to do great things in the world, and I couldn't imagine a man I'd be willing to change my whole life for, a man I'd be willing to give that up for. Then I met you.

"When I came here, my career was in shreds. I was reeling and looking for a safe place to lick my wounds. I may have saved your world, Campbell, but you saved *me.* You gave me the steady, unwavering support I needed to figure out who I was without all the things I'd used to define myself. You saw past the job, past the accomplishments. You saw *me.* You gave me new purpose, and you helped me realize that I didn't have to give anything up. Because you were the man I didn't have to change to be with. You taught me that I could write my own rules for the life I wanted—that I could not only accomplish those great things on my own terms, but I could find more joy and fulfillment than I could possibly imagine, doing them with you by my side. A partner in the truest sense of the word. And I want to spend the rest of our lives adding chapters to that new story, starting with becoming your wife."

Sandy watched her son swallow hard, a manful effort to hold himself together. All around her, Campbell women and others threatened to drown out the rest of the ceremony with their weeping.

They exchanged rings and took their vows —to love, honor, and cherish. And when Reverend Prescott pronounced them man and wife, the entire town cheered.

Cam didn't wait for permission. Grinning, he swept Norah into his arms and back into a dip as he took her mouth.

Reverent Prescott smiled indulgently, and his voice was both wry and amused as he announced, "You may kiss your br—"

The ground began to tremble. A murmur swept through the crowd.

"What on Earth?"

The fountain geysered up, water shooting high into the air and misting the assembly. After one collective gasp—and a few cries of shock—the townspeople watched in stunned silence. No one moved, and not a sound was heard except for the gushing of water. A few moments later, the pressure dropped, and, miraculously, the fountain returned to the happy burble Sandy hadn't heard since Cam was a toddler.

Norah's voice rang out in the quiet. "For the love of all things marketing, somebody tell me you got that shot."

PICTURES HAD BEEN TAKEN, the cake had been cut, the first dance had been had, and the reception had turned into an all-out street party. Walls of all the tents were open to the fine weather and invited guests mingled with the townspeople who'd just shown up to celebrate the First Couple of Wishful. That was what more than one person was calling them. And why not? Who had given more of themselves to the town than the councilman and city planner? But the cheerful crowd and the falling darkness made locating Waylan Crawford damned near impossible.

Trey hadn't seen him at the wedding. Neither had any of the officers from Wishful PD, who'd been circulating as guests. Maybe he'd left. Decided that facing all these people wouldn't be worth it. But that didn't play for Trey. No matter how uninvolved Waylan had been in Cam's life, he simply couldn't imagine the man not wanting to speak to his son on his wedding day.

Since the ceremony itself, he'd stayed within line sight of Sandy as much as possible, without actually catching her attention. They'd had a Moment during the procession. Had she been thinking about their wedding, unconventional though it had been? Had she been missing him? God knew, the past few days he'd felt like he was missing a limb. He didn't quite know what to do with the unreasonable hope that flared in his chest. So, he stayed out of her way—a feat easily accomplished, as she was tied up with mother-of-the-groom duties.

The speeches started. From the dance floor that had been erected near the catering tent, Norah and Cam eloquently thanked the townsfolk for the part they played in making this wedding happen. Trey circled around the edge, weaving through guests. Mitch Campbell gave his best man speech, then passed off the mic to his sister, as the maid of honor.

Kane appeared like some kind of ghost. "No sign."

"You don't really think he's gone, do you?"

"If he is, the feds are gonna be pissed. They've just arrived."

Applause swept the crowd. Miranda handed the microphone to Sandy.

Sandy smiled at her town, and Trey's heart gave a little tug to see it. She looked a little tired, but radiantly happy, and utterly beautiful.

"Like my son and daughter-in-law, I want to say thank you to every single person who pitched in to make this happen. And I want to give a round of applause and say a special thanks to the man who worked tirelessly behind the scenes—"

"Why thank you, honey."

Sandy froze as Waylan melted out of the throng and slipped his arm tight around her waist.

That son of a bitch.

Trey edged closer, his hands curled to fists. The police hesitated at the periphery, and every single Campbell was ready to brawl, but no one moved, waiting to take Sandy's lead. There was no mistaking the death glare she turned on her ex-husband, but she didn't shout, didn't shove, didn't do anything to draw further attention to the wrongness of the situation. Instead, she lowered the mic and spoke in low tones.

Waylan's voice carried. "I just wanted to say a few words to my boy and his bride." He grabbed the microphone from her hand.

"Damn, that's ballsy," Kane muttered.

The bastard's hand was on her. Trey wanted to break it, wanted to twist Waylan's arm behind his back and drop him to his knees. But he remembered what Sandy had said.

I don't need you to ride in like some knight on a charger to come to my rescue.

She wouldn't want a scene, so Trey stayed put, acid churning in his gut.

When Pete took a step forward, Sandy shook her head just once as Waylan began to speak.

"I'm so proud of my boy. My work has kept me traveling, without as much time with my son as I'd have liked, and it's good to see that hereditary Crawford charm served him so well, landing him not only such a pretty bride, but a place on the city council, and the affections of the townspeople, who came together to make this day happen. Good job, son." He gave Norah a salacious wink that had Trey rethinking his position on the sidelines.

The unmitigated gall of the man. To reduce

Norah to a pretty face and Cam's accomplishments and relationship with the town to nothing more than the result of a few glib words.

Across the stage, Cam's hands were bunched into fists, rage written across his face. Norah had him by the arm, murmuring something in low tones. The voice of reason. How much longer would it hold? Trey's own restraint was wearing thin.

Waylan's eyes fixed on something well behind Trey. The feds? His arm tightened around Sandy, and he took a step back, pulling her with him.

"What are you doing?" The mic in Waylan's hand caught her whispered question.

"We need to have a chat," he murmured.

A muscle ticked in Sandy's jaw and she shut her eyes for a moment, as if praying or counting for patience. When she opened them again, her gaze found Trey's. A plea was written clear on her face. But a plea for what? To stay back as she'd always wanted? Or to intervene?

Waylan was starting to tug her off stage.

To hell with it. He wasn't letting this chance go to waste.

Trey stalked onto the empty dance floor, Waylan in his sights. "Get your hands off her." His voice rang out clear in the silence, even without a microphone.

Waylan's eyes went wide with feigned surprise. "What? I'm just having a moment with my wife."

"Ex-wife," Sandy ground out.

At her vehemence, Waylan's expression shifted to true shock. "You wound me, sugar."

"Don't tempt me." Her eyes were spitting fire.

"Let. Her. Go." Trey enunciated each word with the snap of a punch. Dimly, he sensed others crowding in behind him.

Seeing he was outnumbered, Waylan gave an ingratiating, *forgive me* smile as he released Sandy. "Aw now, I didn't mean any harm."

Trey snapped. He surged forward, grabbing Waylan by his lapels and driving him back. The other man stumbled, tried to bring up his hands in defense, but Trey slammed him into a tree.

"No harm? No harm? You pompous, selfish bastard." He yanked Waylan forward and slammed him back again, hard enough to crack his head against the wood.

"Trey, stop! He's not worth it."

Trey turned his head to meet Sandy's stricken eyes. "But you are. You always were. And it's time we ended this."

Her face paled, but she nodded once. It was all the permission Trey needed. He shifted his attention back to Waylan. "All you have ever done is cause harm to the people you were supposed to love most in the world. That stops today. For the rest of your life, you're going to stay far, far away from Sandra and the son you never deserved." He dropped his voice low, leaning in. "And on the off chance that the federal government doesn't see to that, I swear to you that I will. I'm a well-connected man, Waylan. There is no limit to the extent of my reach. Do we understand each other?"

Waylan stared at him. "Who the fuck are you?"

"The man who loves her the way you never did." Trey lifted his voice. "Chief!"

Police Chief Ethan Greer strode up, flanked by a man and woman Trey pegged as out-of-towners on the first glance. "We'll take it from here."

Waylan tensed, his eyes rolling toward the police. "Take what where?"

Trey released his death grip on Waylan's lapels and slapped a faux friendly hand on his shoulder. "There are some folks here who've come a long way to have a conversation with you."

The look of greasy panic that slid over Waylan's face was gratifying.

Trey started to turn away. "Oh, one more thing."

The other man gave him a wary look. "What?"

Trey clocked him, and nothing had ever felt more satisfying than the sing of impact up his arm and down his back. Something crunched beneath his knuckles.

Waylan hit the ground with a howl, both hands covering his face. Blood dripped between his fingers onto the crisp white of his shirt. "You broke my fucking nose!"

"Be glad that's all I broke." He looked toward the feds. "He's all yours."

Sandy's arms were wrapped around her middle, and her cheeks were pale as she watched the officers of Wishful PD close in on her ex-husband. "What's going on? Why are the police here?"

Trey wanted to take her into his arms, to comfort and shield, but he had no idea how she'd take the news. She hadn't wanted him to get involved, and he'd ignored that directive. But he moved close enough his voice wouldn't carry. "To take him in for questioning. He's made some questionable friends the past few years."

She shook her head in disbelief. "How did you even...?"

"I hired a private investigator." He wouldn't apologize for it. At long last, he'd done what needed to be done to get Waylan out of her life for good. Even if it meant losing her.

It was the federal agents who hauled Waylan to his feet, one on either side.

"I'm pressing assault charges!" he shouted. "There are hundreds of witnesses."

There were, indeed. Trey looked around at the gathered crowd, all staring and talking. The whole thing had become exactly the kind of spectacle Sandy abhorred. Well, he'd take responsibility for his actions.

Flexing his aching hand, he turned to Ethan. "I'm not sorry. Do what you need to do."

The police chief glanced around the crowd. "Anybody see anything?"

"Not a thing, Chief."

"Nope."

"Forgot my glasses."

"Anybody know if there's more cake?"

Expression neutral, Ethan turned back to

Waylan. "Looks like you're short some of those witnesses."

"This is an outrage. I'll have your job for this!"

"Be hard to do that from Baltimore," the female agent said. "Get your ass moving."

As the crowd parted to let them through, Ethan looked down at Trey's hand. "You should get some ice on that." Then he fell into step behind the others.

CHAPTER 12

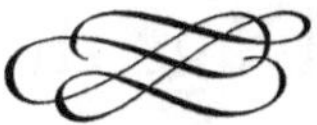

HE'D DISAPPEARED.

AFTER ISSUING a stiff apology to Sandy and the bride and groom, Trey had slipped away. She'd been busy attempting to get the party started again, and when she'd turned around, he was gone. What did that even mean?

"Are you okay?" Cam asked.

Sandy hardly knew. Her ex-husband had just been hauled off by the police—and federal agents, no less! What the hell had he gotten involved in? What had he brought to her town? As the mayor, she wanted to follow their newly minted Chief of Police to find out. As the mother of the groom, she wanted to do whatever she could to salvage the night for her son.

"Are you?" she countered.

"It was a helluva wedding present, seeing him get what he deserved." Cam gave an apologetic shrug. "I know you hate scenes, but it's worth it knowing he's finally pushed too far. I don't think he'll be back."

No. No, Trey had made sure of that.

What did it say about her that part of her had enjoyed seeing him lay Waylan out flat?

She owed Trey an apology and a thank you. She owed him a lot more than that. She'd ignored Waylan, treated him as the irritation he'd always been, and the situation had almost gotten away from her. But even after everything, Trey had been there. He'd stepped in. He'd had her back. And if she'd let him do it sooner, maybe things wouldn't have come to a head in front of the entire town.

Someone had switched the music back on and spectators were beginning to drift back to the party. Sandy knew better than to think anybody would be talking of anything else for weeks, maybe months to come, but she hoped the actual tone of celebration could be reclaimed.

She wished she still felt like celebrating.

Norah slid an arm around her waist. "You should go find him."

Did Trey even want to be found?

"It's your wedding reception," Sandy protested.

"It'll be going for a while yet, I suspect. You'll feel better after you talk to him."

Sandy looked to Cam.

He kissed her cheek. "Go. We're fine here."

Not knowing where else to look, she headed for The Babylon. Louis would probably be there. If she could find him, he could find Trey. Probably. As she passed the fountain, a man fell into step beside her. She tensed. Was he a reporter? Someone connected to Waylan? Someone *after* Waylan?

"Mrs. Peyton."

Sandy stopped dead to get a better look at him and recognized the broad shoulders and big barrel chest. "You. You were at Tosca last night."

"Yes, ma'am."

"You're Trey's detective," she realized.

He inclined his head.

So, Trey had still been protecting her, even when he wasn't with her. And she was surprised to realize she wasn't annoyed by that. She was...warmed by the idea.

"Before you go find him, there's something you should see." He pressed something into her hand.

Sandy stared at the jump drive. What was on here? Whatever dirt he'd managed to dig up on Waylan? "I don't understand." But when she lifted her head, the detective wasn't standing there.

She turned a quick circle, but he was just…gone.

"What the hell?"

"Sandy!" Adele hurried over. "You okay, sugar?"

She curled her fingers around the drive in her hand. "I have a feeling I could use some moral support. Will you come to my office with me?"

"Of course."

In silence, they climbed to the second floor of City Hall. The lights were still on from where the boys had dressed earlier for the wedding. Garment bags and other wedding detritus were scattered everywhere. Sandy picked her way through it and circled around her desk to plug in the flash drive.

Adele crowded beside her. "What's that?"

"We're about to find out."

Inside the single folder was a lone video file. Surveillance footage? She clicked play.

It wasn't surveillance. It wasn't anything to

do with Waylan at all. The screen filled with a garish, neoclassical chapel. Faint strains of "Love Me Tender" spilled out from the speakers as the camera panned toward the front, where Trey stood beside…Elvis, in a gold lame sport jacket, strumming a guitar and crooning out of tune.

"Holy shit. Is this…?"

"My wedding."

Adele leaned closer to the screen. "Where are you?"

"In the back, I guess."

As they watched, Elvis finished his song. Trey's lips twitched with amusement, as he clapped the other man on the shoulder. "Hey, do you mind if I play her down the aisle myself?"

"Whatever floats your boat, brother."

"Thank you. Thank you very much," Trey deadpanned, and made Elvis grin. The camera followed as he slipped behind the white piano set to one side. His fingers stroked over the keys, coaxing out the familiar notes of "Moon River". Sandy's heart squeezed. He'd played her favorite song. Adele wrapped an arm around her shoulders.

The camera swung back up the aisle to where Sandy stood, a bouquet of stargazer lilies in her hands, the glimmer of tears in her eyes. She began the procession, striding without hesitation or stumble toward the front of the chapel. She wasn't drunk. At least not the kind of falling down, black out drunk she'd imagined. She knew what she was doing and who she was walking toward.

Trey finished the song and stood, joining her at the altar in front of Elvis, who beamed a crooked smile at them both.

"You two crazy kids ready for this?"

On the screen, Sandy handed her flowers off to an attendant and slipped her hands into Trey's. In that moment—when her inhibitions were lowered; when she hadn't been a single mom trying to prove she could do everything; when she wasn't Mayor Crawford, with a reputation to uphold; when she'd let all the other crap go and she was just Sandy—she'd looked at

Trey like he held the moon. And he looked back at her like he'd just handed it over with a big red bow.

"Yes," they chorused.

In her office, with her best friend beside her, she whispered, "I married him because I wanted to."

"Yeah, looks like you did."

As she watched herself on screen, beaming at her new husband, she thought back to what Cam said about learning to love a strong woman and how he'd said partnership didn't make Norah incapable or less. If Norah had believed that it did, if she'd pushed Cam away for trying to help and support her, Sandy would've been bitterly disappointed in her. What did it say about Sandy that she hadn't held herself to the same standard?

She sank into her chair. "I think I've made a huge mistake."

"Marrying him?"

"In how I treated him after." Sandy scooped a hand through her hair. "I told him I wanted to give our marriage a real chance, but at the first sign of trouble, I reverted to what I've always done. Pushing him away and insisting I could handle things myself. The truth is, I've never truly given him a place in my life. In college, I couldn't let him be more than a friend because I wasn't free."

"Appropriate."

"Except he wasn't ever just a friend." She'd made him a lover in all but body and kept him perpetually on the sidelines. "I took advantage of his strength and the comfort he offered when I needed it, and never let him act on his need to protect me. And here it is, thirty years later, and I did the same damned thing."

She'd accepted the parts of him she'd wanted—the kisses, the touches, the smiles, and laughter—the easy parts that felt natural and good. But she'd rejected his need to protect her. She'd kept him on the sidelines—again. Relegated him to secrecy and made him a shadow in her life—again. Because she hadn't changed at all.

Miserably, Sandy lifted her gaze to Adele's. "I owe him more than that. I owe him everything. And I'm afraid I've screwed it all up."

Adele kicked back against the desk and crossed her arms. "Given that display at the reception—which, I've gotta say, was really hot in an alpha male badass kind of way—I don't think the situation is irreparable."

God, Sandy hoped not.

"The question is, what are you prepared to do to fix it?"

By Monday the green was back to normal. The event tents had been packed away and the dance floor dismantled. The only remaining evidence of the weekend's festivities were the twinkle lights still wrapped around the trees. And, no doubt, the lingering gossip at Dinner Belles and The Grind.

Trey had never intended to bring any more disgrace on Sandy. Yet he couldn't regret finally having the chance to act, to finish things with Crawford, once and for all. According to Kane, the bastard had been flown back to Baltimore yesterday. There were talks of plea bargains and relocation instead of jail time. Either way, she would be safe from him. Finally.

Maybe it was foolish to end his stay in Wishful back at the fountain. Trey certainly hadn't gotten the wish he'd made—for the life he'd always wanted with Sandy. She'd warned him, hadn't she? That you had to be careful what you wished for. Maybe it had been too selfish a wish. He'd meant it to be about them, but it had really been about him and finally getting resolution. Trey supposed he'd gotten that, in a way. Still, he was here to do better by her before he left town.

Clutching the quarter tight in his hand, he stared at the freely running water of the fountain.

I wish for Sandy's happiness, in whatever form that may take.

He kissed the coin and tossed it in. The

thunk was lost in the soft roar of the water. Well, that was it then.

A car screeched to a stop on Market Street. Like everyone else out and about on the green, Trey looked to see what was going on. Louis leapt out of the driver's seat. Trey stared in shock as his unflappable executive assistant began to run across the green as if the hounds of hell were on his heels.

The other man's hair was mussed, his eyes just a little bit wild, as he skidded to a stop beside the fountain. "Sir, I…didn't know what the appropriate thing was. Maybe I should have called right away, but it seemed like something that should be handled in person…given the… the personal nature…"

Had Louis had some kind of family emergency? "Slow down, man. What the hell are you talking about?"

Louis just hit a button and handed over the tablet he carried.

A video played in the browser. And holy shit, there Trey was with Sandy. And Elvis.

Damn, it really hadn't been a dream. Here was their wedding in living color. Trey's heart warmed. They looked so damned happy taking their vows. But his instinctive grin faded as his gaze tracked up to the header of the site hosting the video.

The 'Berg: Everything worth knowing in Wishful.

Oh God. Their Vegas wedding was posted on the town's gossip blog. This was a disaster for Sandy. Everyone would know about their hasty marriage. What would this do to her reputation as mayor? He had to do something.

"Shut it down," he commanded Louis. "Whatever it takes. I don't care if you have to cut off power to the whole damned town until you can get it gone."

"But sir, the internet is forev—"

Trey didn't hear the rest as he bolted for City Hall, already noticing the eyes following him, the pointing fingers.

Damn it. *Damn it.* He didn't want this for her. He'd been trying to respect her wishes on this at least. How the hell had they gotten hold of the video?

Trey raced past old Jerry Noble at the metal detector.

"Mr. Peyton?"

"Sorry, Jerry. Gotta see the Mayor." He bypassed the elevator and sprinted up the stairs.

Avery looked up, startled as he hit the vestibule. "Mr. Peyton. Good morning. She's—"

He burst into Sandy's office.

"—in."

From her desk, his wife looked up, eyes going wide. "Trey."

He shut the door in Avery's face. He'd apologize to her later. They needed privacy for this. "I'm sorry. I'm so sorry. I don't know how it happened. The video was supposed to be locked in my safe. But I swear to you my lawyers and I will put a stop to this. I don't care what they say about how the internet is forever. I'll find a way to get this cleaned up."

She just blinked at him. Why didn't she look

more upset? Oh, dear God. Did she not know about it yet?

Sandy rose and came around the desk. "I'm sorry. If I'd known you were going to feel this strongly about it, I never would have leaked the video."

"Of course, I—Wait." His whole world came to a screeching halt and flipped upside down. "What?"

"I'm the one who leaked the video of our wedding."

"You? But…why?"

"I thought it made a statement."

A statement? It sure as hell did. It told everyone in town that they'd had a quickie wedding in an Elvis wedding chapel.

A beat later, something else sank in: It told everyone in town that they were married.

She'd taken ownership of their marriage. She'd put aside her pride and let everyone in on the truth in the most public way possible.

Her computer chirped.

Trey was still staring at her when she circled back around to check it.

"Oh, Cam's Skyping me." She twisted the screen so he could see, then perched on the desk as she answered the call. "Hi, honey! Are y'all enjoying your honeymoon?"

"So not why we called," Cam said. A fist shot out to thump him in the shoulder. "Ow."

Norah came into the frame. "We wanted to congratulate you."

Sandy beamed. "Thank you, sweetheart."

"I don't understand. *When* exactly did you... um...elope?" Cam asked.

"The weekend before your wedding. We waited thirty years and thought that was quite long enough but the least we could do was hold off until after your wedding to announce it. Of course, I'd have done it more subtly, but somebody got ahold of the video and, well...I'm guessing you've seen it."

Cam arched a brow. "So...you're okay with that?"

Her lips curved in wry amusement. "Well,

nobody can ever accuse me of being stodgy and boring, now can they?"

Her son remained skeptical. "And…you're happy?"

The eyes she turned on Trey were warm. "This time I made the right choice."

His heart just squeezed. She'd chosen him. At long last, she'd chosen him.

Throat thick with emotion, Trey sat on the opposite side of the desk, sliding an arm around her shoulders and pressing his brow to hers. "I'll take care of her," he promised. "And I'll love her 'til the day I die."

On a sigh, Sandy wrapped her arms around him, and his world righted itself again.

Norah sniffed. "Awww. I'm so happy for y'all."

"I owe you my thanks. If not for you, I'd never have come back to Wishful."

"We'll chalk it up to the happy circularity of Fate," she said.

"You hate the idea of Fate," Cam pointed out.

"Maybe I'm changing my mind." She gave her husband a smacking kiss. "We're going to let y'all go. See you in two weeks!"

"Enjoy St. John's." Sandy disconnected.

"You told them. You told everybody."

"I did."

The phone in Trey's pocket buzzed. Louis with an update on the take down? He slipped it out. "From Tess. 'Dad. Call me.' Looks like it's my turn to spread the good news."

"Do you want to do that on your own, or should we do that together?"

He set the phone aside and scooped her up, hauling her across the desk and into his lap. "I think we should do everything together. Forever."

"I'm good with that." She looped her arms around him. "Maybe we could start with a proper honeymoon?"

Oh yeah, he was all over that. He wondered how long she could get off work. "Where do you want to go?"

Sandy considered for a moment. "I've always wanted to see Paris."

"Then you, Mrs. Peyton, shall have the City of Lights. And anything else your heart desires."

Sandy lifted her mouth to his. "I just need you."

And that, Trey decided, as he kissed his wife, made him the richest man in the world.

Choose Your Next Romance!

NEXT UP IN the Wishful line up is a heartwarming, Hallmark-style Christmas story—with a little bit of heat. Mary Alice Reed is a woman done wrong. Don't you just know when she swears off men, she finally finds Mr. Right? Come meet Dr. McHottie in *The Christmas Fountain*.

If you'd like to finally meet Trey's daughter Tess, jump on ahead to *You Were Meant For Me*. This one is a vacation fling, accidental pregnancy romance that's going to absolutely ROCK the family. I recommend popcorn.

Looking for more big-hearted billionaires? Also included in this volume is a bonus read —*Once Upon An Heirloom,* a Meet Cute Romance.

A blind date on Valentine's Day. What could possibly go wrong?

After being duped and robbed by a charming ex-boyfriend, Sylvie Noll is forced to go to a jewelry store to sell a beloved family heirloom or lose the business she's put everything into.

Everett William Sperry, III is a hard-core do-gooder with a heart of gold and bank account to back him up. He impulsively buys Sylvie's hocked ring, intent on returning it to her. But Sylvie disappears.

How will he find her again? And if his friends find his grand gestures...eccentric, how will a complete stranger react?

The sidewalks were packed with people. Crowds moved in steady streams in and out of the shops lining the cobbled streets, juggling bags and packages. In general, they moved with frenzied purpose and a serious lack of holiday spirit. As he wove his way through them, Everett William Sperry, III wondered why in God's name Brandon felt the need to meet at the Taproom in the midst of all the holiday crazy. This is what on-line shopping is for. To *avoid* this insanity. Also to avoid all the bell ringers, because he had absolutely no defense against them and felt compelled to drop a substantial donation into every charity bucket he passed. But Brandon had declared a state of emergency, so Everett had come.

Snow swirled from the pewter sky in fat, wet flakes, sticking to his lashes, his clothes, rapidly slushing up the street of the massive outdoor mall. The hike back to his car when this was over was going to be lots of fun. Everett hunched his shoulders against the bitter wind blowing down from the mountain and picked up the pace. The sooner he got there, the sooner he'd thaw out.

Up ahead, someone burst out of the Rocky Mountain Chocolate Factory, flinging the door wide and barreling onto the sidewalk. A middle-aged woman in a puffy pink coat jerked to a halt in an effort to avoid being smacked in the face by the door. The abrupt motion had her feet sliding, the arms full of bags beginning to pinwheel. Everett leapt forward, skidding, and reached for her. The bags went flying, but he managed to catch the woman before she hit the cold, hard ground. The man who'd come out of the chocolate shop never even noticed, already halfway down the block with a cell phone pressed to his ear.

Nothing like Christmas to bring out the Grinch in people, he thought.

Planting his feet, Everett righted the woman. "You okay?"

"Oh my gracious." She laid a hand over her heart. "You saved me from a broken tail bone at the least."

"Least I could do. Nobody wants to spend Christmas sitting on a donut. Here, let me help you with that." Everett knelt and gathered up the scattered purchases.

"Thank you, young man," she said, accepting the collection of bags. "Somebody clearly raised you right."

He flashed a smile. "My mama will be happy to hear it. You have a merry Christmas, now." Everett waited a minute, watching to make sure his rescuee really had her footing back before continuing the remaining couple of blocks to the Taproom.

The moment he stepped inside, his face and hands began to sting from the heat. Stomping the snow from his boots, he scanned the room, looking for his friend. Brandon sat at the bar, thumbing his phone.

Stripping off the damp layers, Everett crossed to him. "Okay, I'm here. What's the emergency?"

"I need your help with something," said Brandon, kicking out the stool beside him. "Sit down. Have a drink."

Everett draped his coat over the back and sank down onto the stool, loosening his scarf. Because he was frozen through, he asked for coffee instead of a beer. "I swear, if you've dragged me out in this mess to help you with your Christmas shopping, I'm going to murder you."

"Not exactly," said Brandon. His hand drummed the bar in rhythm with the jazzy version of "Jingle Bell Rock" playing in the background. His cheeks were faintly flushed and his mouth seemed to be at war between deadly serious and goofy grin.

"I'm guessing by your expression that nobody died, so what's going on?" Everett nodded thanks to the bartender as she filled a mug to the brim.

The grin won the war. "I'm going to propose to Isabelle."

Everett waited a beat as that sank in, then grinned himself. "Dude, that's awesome!" He clapped Brandon on the back. The little brunette had kept his friend besotted for nearly a year now. They were great together. "Am I here to help you plan the thing? Some kind of epic surprise? Will there be a flash mob? We should get Travis in on this."

Brandon lifted a brow. "Flash mob? Do I need to be investigating your YouTube viewing history in order to stage an intervention?"

"I blame my mother. She keeps sending me videos of these epic proposals. I don't know if she thinks this is going to prompt me to find a woman or what. Anyway, if you need a plan, I'm your man."

Brandon waved that away. "No, no, I'm fine on the how. Or I will be. Still working on that. And Travis is on his way. I want your help in picking out a ring."

"My help?" asked Everett. "Not that I'm not flattered to be asked, but why?"

"Well, apart from the fact that this is a big step and I want my closest friends with me when I do it, I want you there because you know about this stuff."

"'This stuff,'" he repeated.

"Jewelry. Diamonds and stuff," Brandon clarified.

"And I know about this how? Because I've got a generational suffix after my name?"

"Because with that blue-blooded upbringing of yours, you've been exposed to the real deal. You know quality when you see it. And you know how to use that eyepiece thing jewelers use."

"A loupe," offered Everett, picking up the

coffee, warming his hands.

"Yeah, that. This is a big deal. I've gotta get it right."

The door opened again and Travis walked in on a swirl of snow and frigid air. He strode over. "Sorry I'm late. What's going on?"

"Brandon here is looking to follow in your footsteps," said Everett.

"Huh?"

"I'm asking Isabelle to marry me."

Travis whooped. "This calls for a celebration!"

"Save the celebration for when she says yes," said Brandon. "We're going ring shopping."

"Want me to call Alicia for a female opinion on this consult?" asked Travis.

"Absolutely not. This is man's work," said Brandon. "There's some kind of unwritten rule or something that you lose points if you need a girl consult."

"Besides, I'm supposed to know about these things," Everett put in.

"Well, alright then," said Travis. "Finish your

drinks and let's get to work."

~

As she paced in front of Vandevelde Jewelers, Sylvie Noll cursed Neal Harrier eight ways from Sunday for being a lying, sneaky, yellow coward dog scumbag. Then she chastised herself for insulting the dog.

How could I have been so stupid *to have been taken in by that cretin?* she wondered.

Because he'd wined and dined her, lowering her defenses with charm and gifts, giving every impression he was a privileged jetsetter. And she'd bought it, hook, line, and sinker. Damn it, she'd been flattered and dazzled by his good looks, unable to imagine that someone like him would be interested in someone like her.

Idiot.

When he said he wanted access to her kitchen to cook her a special meal for their three month anniversary, she'd thought, *Oh, how sweet*, and given him a key.

Moron.

He cleaned her out. TV. Laptop. Jewelry. The Christmas presents she'd bought to mail home to her family in Alabama. The deposit from the gallery that she hadn't taken to the bank the night before because of the crappy weather. Every single thing of value in her apartment. He'd even found her rainy day emergency stash in the toe of her favorite boots.

Of course, Sylvie had called the cops. They'd taken her statement, cataloged her missing things. And informed her that the bastard had done the exact same thing to three other women. They were still looking, but the investigating officer surmised that Neal—who'd used other aliases with the other victims—had probably blown town. He suggested that she file a claim on her renters' insurance.

Right. The renters' insurance she didn't have because she hadn't been able to afford it.

She was, in a word, screwed.

At least the bastard hadn't gotten keys to the

gallery and hadn't been able to access the stock. Now next month's rent was almost due on her apartment *and* the shop, and her landlords were not what you could call sympathetic to her plight. She'd have to move out of the apartment. There was no question of that. But she had to find a way to save her gallery.

The only thing Sylvie had left that was worth anything was her grandmother's engagement ring, which she habitually wore on a chain around her neck. She thanked God that the bastard hadn't gotten away with it, too. It was the only thing she had left of her grandmother. And it could mean the difference between saving the life she'd built here and conceding defeat and slinking home to Alabama as a failure.

If she could make herself go inside.

But how could she part with it? What would Mawmaw say?

Sylvie, my girl, it's just jewelry. I believed in you when you decided to head out to Colorado in the first place. If this ring will help save you, don't let a little thing like sentiment hold you back. Think of it as me giving you another little boost.

"Easy for you to say," Sylvie muttered.

The door of Vandevelde's opened and a man stuck his head out, a polite, but wary expression on his face. "Can I help you, ma'am? Do you need directions?"

Sylvie jolted and looked around. But, no, he was talking to her. She realized she probably looked like a crazy person trying to decide whether to rob the store.

"Oh! I…no. That is, I don't need directions."

It's now or never, girl.

She braced herself. "And yes, you can help me. I have a ring I was hoping you could take a look at."

The man's face relaxed and he held the door open wider. "Certainly. Please, come in."

Sylvie stepped out of the December cold and into the hushed space of the shop. It wasn't a huge room but the air somehow felt heavy and kind of reverent, like a museum. Glass cases ran in a U along the sides and back, with room for the jeweler behind. He stepped through a little half door into his arena and pulled a pair of bifocals from his shirt front pocket.

"Now, what can I do for you, Miss?"

With only a moment's hesitation, Sylvie pulled the necklace from her sweater and removed the ring. Gently, she handed it over. "It was my grandmother's."

The jeweler took it, examining the art deco setting. "It's lovely craftsmanship."

"I've always loved all the filigree. It seems so classy and elegant. Like she was." As he examined it, Sylvie continued to talk. "She was an actress back in her day. Stage productions, mostly. Tallulah Bankhead was a cousin and helped her get her start up in New York. Mawmaw loved the stage, all the lights and the applause. When she met my granddaddy, she was headlining in *America's Sweetheart* on Broadway. He swept her off her feet. So much so that they were married in less than two months, and he gave her this ring. Granddad always used to say that was how he stole America's sweetheart for his own."

The jeweler smiled. "That's a lovely story."

Sylvie flushed. "Sorry. I tend to go on a bit."

"S'fine. It's nice to know the history of a piece." He peered at her over the glasses. "None of the stones seem to be loose. Did you need it resized?"

"She absolutely had smaller fingers than I do. Wore a five. Tiny, tiny hands." *You're babbling,* she chided herself. *Get to the point.* "The fact is, I'm looking to sell it."

"Oh? Seems like an important piece to you."

"It is. You have no idea."

The door opened, interrupting the quiet with the noise of foot traffic outside. Sylvie glanced over to see a trio of men walk in.

"I'll be with you gentlemen in a bit," said the jeweler.

One lifted his hand. "No rush. We'll just look around."

Sylvie turned back to the counter.

"You were looking to sell?" he prompted.

"Oh, yes. Well, I'm in a terrible financial bind. I made the mistake of trusting the wrong person, and I—well, you don't need all the gory details—but it's bad, and this is the only thing I have left. I don't *want* to sell it, but I really don't have a choice."

"I see."

"I came here because you have a reputation for fair pricing. And I swear I'm not making all this up like some kind of sob story to make you feel sorry for me. I'd never do that. I just— sorry, I tend to over share."

The jeweler took off the glasses and laid them on the counter.

Sylvie's heart sank. He wasn't going to buy it. She'd be forced to go to a pawn shop, where she'd get pennies on the dollar for what it was actually worth. But the jeweler merely picked up a loupe and began to examine the stones. As her stomach knotted, Sylvie clasped her hands and resigned herself to waiting, while this man determined whether she'd sink or have the chance to keep on swimming.

Everett paused in front of a case of watches and tried to look like he wasn't shamelessly eavesdropping. It was a terrible compulsion, but the moment she'd mentioned she was in financial trouble, he couldn't help but tune in.

She was southern. A drawl underscored the earnest tone as she tried to correct whatever impression she thought she'd given. As the jeweler picked up a loupe to examine the stones in the ring, Everett glanced over at the woman. She wore a good quality red parka, worn but good boots, and seemed properly dressed for the weather. Her blonde hair was pulled back in a loose braid. It gave him a clear view of her profile and the spots of color riding high in her cheeks. Embarrassment. *And some anxiety*, he thought, catching sight of the hands she was wringing as she waited.

What had brought her so low that she was selling a piece that clearly meant a lot to her?

"What do you think of this one over here?"

"Huh?" Everett turned his attention to Brandon, crossing to a case on the other side to see what he was pointing out. "No, not marquis. Isabelle has little hands. You want something more delicate. Princess or round."

The jeweler finished his inspection. "It's certainly an exquisite piece and there's a market for antique rings, but you must understand, I won't be your best bet for maximizing profit."

"You have a business to run and access to wholesale markets. I get that."

"I wouldn't ordinarily bring this up, but given your unique circumstance, I feel I should. I have a colleague down in Denver who deals in consignment. He has a generous 70/30 split of the sale price. With the current market, you'd do considerably better going that route."

"I appreciate your honesty, but I'm not in a position to wait, and I don't have a way to get to Denver at the moment. What's the best you can do?"

Everett shifted so he could see the woman as she took the slip of paper the jeweler offered.

Her eyes closed after she read it and she swallowed once, hard.

"I'm sorry it can't be more."

Though she looked pained, the woman nodded. "Let's do it."

"I'll put together the paperwork."

As the jeweler disappeared to an office in the back, the woman knuckled away tears and picked up the ring. "I'm sorry," she whispered.

Travis elbowed him. "Earth to Everett. How about checking back in to this planet and offering up some opinions."

"Sorry, sorry."

As they debated the merits of white gold versus platinum, simple versus ornate, half of Everett's mind was on the woman.

I trusted the wrong person.

Who would take advantage of such a sweet soul? Or maybe that was exactly it. Somebody thought she'd make a good mark. And evidently she had if she was in deep enough to be here. He wished he could do something to help.

As the jeweler re-emerged, paperwork in

hand, Brandon called out, "When you get a minute, we've got a few engagement rings we'd like to see."

"Be right with you."

"Dude, what's up with you?" whispered Brandon.

"Nothing. I just couldn't help overhearing." He nodded toward the woman.

"Yeah. Sucky situation all around," conceded Brandon. "Nothing you can do about it, though. Even if there was, she's gone now."

Everett whipped around in time to see her striding out the door, heading west.

"What can I help you gentlemen with?" inquired the jeweler, coming around to their side of the store.

Travis slapped Brandon on the back. "My buddy here is looking to get himself hitched."

"Congratulations, sir. What sort of ring are you in the market for?"

"Actually, can we see the one you just bought?" asked Everett.

"Certainly." The jeweler retrieved it.

Brandon held it up. "I don't know. It looks pretty small. Isabelle's tiny, but not *that* tiny."

"We can resize anything that isn't the correct size."

"May I?" Everett held out a hand. The round cut sapphire was flanked by smaller accent diamonds in an ornate, antique setting.

"The story that came with it was rather sweet. Her grandmother was a Broadway star back in her day. Had a whirlwind romance with the grandfather and with this ring, he stole America's sweetheart."

A story like that made this a real part of a family history. An heirloom. Everett had been taught to respect and value such things. He suspected from the seller's level of upset that she had, as well. Which made the situation that much more tragic. The ring itself was a lovely piece, but it could've been hideous and he still would've asked, "How much?"

"Wait a minute," protested Brandon. "I haven't even looked at these others. And I think she'd prefer a traditional diamond."

"Not for you," said Everett. "How much?"

The jeweler named a figure.

Everett didn't blink. "Ring it up."

"Man, what the hell are you doing?" asked Brandon.

"My good deed for the year. If you could ring it up fast, that would be great."

"Everett, buddy, are you about to do what I think you're about to do?" asked Travis. He kept his voice light and even, the kind of tone you used with a person threatening to jump off a ledge.

"I have no idea what you think I'm about to do." Everett handed over his credit card.

"I think you're about to buy an engagement ring for a perfect stranger."

"Then yes, I'm doing exactly what you think I'm doing."

"This is insane," said Brandon.

"Life's too short not to be a little crazy once in a while. Besides, it's not like I'm proposing. I just want to give it back to her." Everett signed the credit card receipt and accepted the ring in a box. Saluting his friends, he said, "I'll be right back!"

He bolted out of Vandevelde's and headed the direction the woman had turned, eyes searching for the red parka and blonde hair. The slushy sidewalks kept him from sprinting, so he took the opportunity to glance through storefront windows. Given the apparently dire state of her finances, Everett didn't figure she'd have been stopping in any of them to shop, but he didn't want to risk missing her. It should've been easy, even with the crowd, but he didn't see her.

She had a five minute head start. How far could she have gotten?

Everett went all the way to the parking area, but there was no sign of the woman who'd sold the ring.

I'll just get her name from the jeweler. He'll have a record from the sale, he thought.

Back at Vandevelde's, Brandon and Travis had narrowed it down to three choices.

"Find her?" asked Travis.

"No," Everett admitted. He looked to the man behind the counter. "Can I get her name and number to arrange a meeting to give the ring back to her?"

"I'm afraid I have a policy of strict confidentiality of my client's information."

Everett tried a smile. "But surely you could make an exception this one time. In the name of a good cause."

"Young man, you may be as well intentioned as you seem. Or you could just as easily be a potential thief or worse. That young lady has had enough trouble in her life. I won't be the cause of more."

Everett tamped down on his disappointment. "No, it's all right. I understand."

"So what are you going to do?" asked Brandon.

"Keep looking. It's doubtful she'd have had any knowledge of the store's reputation if she wasn't a local. Town's just not that big. I'll run into her eventually." Everett moved over to the counter. "Now, let's see those contenders."

"The groundhog lied," declared Brenna, plunking down into a chair. "There is absotively no evidence of spring out there."

Sylvie smiled at her new roommate and speared a chip into the bowl of queso. "You do realize that Punxsutawney Phil has absolutely *no* bearing on whether we're getting spring early or having more winter, right?"

"Spare me the lecture and gimme some of that cheese dip. God, it's freezing."

Sylvie shoved the basket of chips closer. "There's something wrong when the southerner isn't the one bitching about the cold."

"I am from *Tucson*," Brenna protested.

"Fair enough. At least we do get a little snow in Huntsville."

"I rest my case." She paused when the waiter arrived to take her drink order and asked for a margarita. "How were things at the gallery today?"

"Good. I'm nearly finished setting up for the

Baudelaire showing that starts next week. And while I was uncrating his paintings, somebody wandered in and bought a sculpture by Lily Birdsong."

"Oh yeah? Which one?"

"The steampunk pygmy owl."

"I *loved* that one!" exclaimed Brenna. "He reminded me of Pigwidgeon from *Harry Potter*."

"A small piece, but a really nice sale," said Sylvie. "And the buyer absolutely had his eye on her copper hawk. I think there's a good chance he may be back."

The server returned with Brenna's margarita, which she immediately lifted in a toast. "This calls for celebration!"

Sylvie clinked her glass to Brenna's.

Things were better. So much better than she could have anticipated at Christmas, when everything seemed to be falling apart. She'd moved out of her apartment and into the stock room at the gallery. Sylvie hadn't slept much during those weeks, constantly worried her landlord would find out and she'd be booted from that space too. Then Brenna, one of the Western artists Sylvie featured in her gallery, had found out about her plight and immediately offered up her spare room. With the sale of the ring and the padding of some post Christmas sales at the gallery, she'd been able to keep her head above water. As a special bonus, Sylvie ended up making a new BFF, something she hadn't managed during her first two backbreaking years in Colorado. She'd always liked Brenna, but living in close quarters had showed her a soul sister.

Neal still hadn't been caught, but things were looking up.

Conversation flowed free and easy over chips and queso, shifting from art to the latest episode of *Iron Chef,* to the current romantic comedy in the theaters.

"We should go this weekend," Brenna declared. "Adam practically broke out in hives the last time I suggested a romcom. I swear, the man doesn't understand that sappy movies totally prime me for *other activities* he'd totally be into."

Sylvie snickered. "His loss."

"Damn straight," Brenna agreed. "So when are you getting back out there?"

"Back out where?"

"Duh. The dating pool."

"Oh, I don't know…a quarter after never?" suggested Sylvie.

"Come on, Syl. You can't stay off the market forever just because one guy turned out to be a stinker."

"He was more than a stinker."

"Okay, yeah, he was a total reprobate," Brenna admitted.

"Reprobate?"

"Asswipe?"

"That works."

"But not all guys are like that."

"You'll forgive me if I don't trust my judgment at the moment."

"If you won't trust your judgment, trust a system."

"A system?"

"Sure. You should try online dating."

"How about hell no?" suggested Sylvie.

"Wait, wait. Hear me out. Perfect Chemistry does background checks on all the people who sign up. And you have to provide a social security number to prove you are who you say you are and that you don't have a criminal record, so nobody can go in and just make up an alias. Their whole system is set up on some kind of psychological matchmaking research, so you're *bound* to do better than by chance."

"Is that how you met Adam of the won't watch your favorite kind of movie persuasion?" Sylvia asked.

"I said *better* than by chance, not perfect," Brenna qualified. "But seriously, despite some flaws, Adam's pretty awesome. And I had good dates with a handful of others before I started going out with him."

Knowing her friend wasn't about to let this go, Sylvie sighed and conceded. "Fine. I'll consider it."

Brenna's dimples flashed.

"What?" asked Sylvie. "I recognize that impish look. What did you do?"

All innocence, Brenna studied her pink, glitter polish-coated nails. "I might have set up a profile for you already. And you might already have some matches in your inbox wanting to talk."

"Brenna!"

"What? You weren't going to act on your own. I'm just giving you a little nudge out of the nest."

"A boot to the ass is more like it," Sylvie grumbled.

"Just look at their profiles. Talk to a few of them. There's absolutely no rule that says you have to actually go out with anybody. But it won't hurt you to dip a toe back in."

The idea of having *somebody* screen dates *was* kind of appealing. And Lord knew she'd been working her butt off since Christmas. It wouldn't be a bad thing to have a little fun. "Well okay," said Sylvie. "Just remember, if something goes sideways and I end up with another Neal, this was all *your* idea."

Brenna clapped in delight. "Excellent! Hurry up and finish your fajitas. I want to go home and check your profile."

"Exactly *why* are you so pumped about this?"

"Apart from the fact that my stake in this is ultimately potential double date material, I'll get vicarious thrills from watching you squirm."

Sylvie's lips curved in a wry smile. "You're a real Saint."

"I thought we were doing Mexican," said Everett.

"The bride-to-be wanted hibachi," explained Brandon as he wheeled into the parking lot of the local Japanese steakhouse. "When she surfaces from an edit, she eats like a stevedore. I've learned not to argue."

From the passenger seat, Isabelle shot him

an affectionate look. "You're just weirded out by the fact that I can out eat you."

"Well, you're half my size," he remarked. "I don't know where you put it."

The pair continued their teasing banter all the way inside. Everett followed, grinning. He liked the way they were together, liked what they brought out in each other.

Brandon asked for a table for three. As they followed the hostess, Everett's gaze swept the restaurant, automatically checking for that blonde hair, as had become his habit over the past weeks. But she wasn't here. Just as she hadn't been anywhere else he'd been since she'd walked out of Vandevelde's. He pocketed the ring box he'd been compulsively juggling in his palm and sat.

"Why are you still toting that thing around?" asked Brandon. "It's been nearly two months. You ought to go sell it back or put it on consignment somewhere. Get some of your money back."

"Money's not the point," said Everett. "This

is a piece of her family history. She deserves to have it back."

"Well, I think it's sweet and romantic," said Isabelle.

"You would," Brandon said, tugging lightly at the end of her pony tail.

"Romance wasn't what I had in mind when I did it," insisted Everett. "I just wanted to do something nice for somebody in a bad spot."

"You've made a career doing nice stuff for people in bad spots," Brandon pointed out. "That would be the entire point of your non-profit, remember?"

Everett waved that off. "That's different."

"You're probably lucky you haven't found this woman. She'd probably take one look at you, recognize you for the blue blood with the biggest, squishiest heart in all of Colorado, and take you to the cleaners."

Everett jerked a thumb at him and looked at Isabelle. "You sure you want to marry this cynic?"

"I'm making it my mission in life to convert

him," she said. "What have you done to track her down?"

"Well, Mr. Vandevelde was understandably reluctant to give me her information on the front end. Confidentiality and all that. And he was absolutely right. I went back later and had him call to try and set up a meeting at the store, but the number she'd given on her paperwork was no longer in service. Since then, I've been mostly back to square one."

"With the number disconnected, she's probably not even still *here*," said Brandon.

Isabelle elbowed him in the ribs. "Ye of little faith. Is there anything you have to go on? Would he give you her name?"

Everett shook his head. "And that's fair too. Somebody had taken awful advantage of her to put her in the position to sell the ring in the first place. He has no way of knowing I wouldn't do the same. I've gotta respect that. But it makes things difficult."

"I think you need to get out there and look for a real woman instead of holding out for some girl you're never going to see again," Brandon insisted.

"I'm not holding out for her," Everett protested. "I didn't do this with some motive of wrangling a date out of it. That would be unethical."

Brandon just arched a brow. "Have you been out with anybody since you bought that thing?"

"Well, no. But things were busy with the holidays, and January is always a busy month at work, and I…" He trailed off at his friend's bland stare.

Maybe he *had* avoided seeking out a date since December. But the search for his mystery woman had captured his imagination. How would a potential date react if he talked about it, as he inevitably would? What normal guy did what he'd done? No normal guy was the truth of it. Normal guys didn't have the discretionary income to indulge in such a crazy gesture.

"I think you've built her up in your mind," said Brandon. "Got this whole damsel in distress thing going on and you the knight in armor and all that. It's a thing with you, that whole addiction to rescuing people."

"So long as he's not taking crazy risks with life and limb, I don't see how that's a bad addiction," countered Isabelle. "Though I can see how that might put you in a position to be taken advantage of yourself."

Brandon threw out a hand in a *See?* gesture. "Thank you."

Everett glared. "I'm hardly some bumbling rube without an ounce of common sense."

"No, you're just determined to see the best in people." Brandon held up a hand for peace before Everett could respond. "I'm not saying there's anything wrong with that. But not everybody's as nice as you."

"So let me get this straight. I'm supposed to give up on finding the woman who sold this ring, stop being nice to everybody, and go out and find somebody to date?"

"I never said you should stop being nice to people. But yeah, I think you need to come to grips with the fact you may never find this woman."

"Well, I've got an alternative plan," said Isabelle.

Everett lifted his sake. "I'm game to hear it."

"You know how when you're looking for something and can't find it, it's not until you stop looking and go do something else that it pops up? Maybe you going out with somebody else will work like that for you. And if it doesn't, then you still might meet Miss Right."

"You happily engaged couples keep trying to marry everybody off," accused Everett.

Isabelle laid a hand over his. "We just want to see you happy."

Everett sighed. "It's hard to argue with that."

She smiled. "You should check out online dating. My friend Leah met her guy through Perfect Chemistry. And indirectly, that's how I met Brandon."

"Fine. I concede your point. I've tried every-thing else, so I might as well try *not* looking and see what happens."

"I don't believe you," said Brandon.

"No? Fine. Just to prove my seriousness, I will sit here and fill out the stinking profile from my phone for your approval."

It took a while between juggling conversation, ordering, eating the soup and salad, but by the time the chef was done with their little show, Everett had finished. He handed the phone over. "There. See?"

"Good man. Now let's see what kind of matches the site comes up with."

Everett rolled his eyes as Brandon began playing with the screen.

"It's given you seven matches right off."

"Possibly because they are the only available women in our area, in the age range, who have profiles on the site," suggested Everett.

Brandon ignored that. "Let's see. There's Anne. Age 26. Oooh, a red-head veterinarian. You're an animal lover. That could be a good pair. Then there's Lina. She's a brunette. Age 30. She's a ski instructor." He tapped some more. "Oh, here we go. This one is an art lover with an addiction to Mexican food. Quite a looker, too." Brandon passed the phone back.

And there she was, staring out at him from the screen. It was a three/quarters profile shot. Casual. Someone had caught her on the verge of a smile as she stood on a trail somewhere in the red parka he'd been looking for all this time. Her eyes were hazel, long-lashed and bracketed by laugh lines.

"Holy shit," breathed Everett.

"What?" asked Brandon.

"I didn't think it would actually work." He looked up. "This is her."

"Wait, seriously?" asked Isabelle, leaning over to peer at the phone. "That's totally not how I thought it would work. I figured you'd go out with somebody else and run into her somewhere. Not that she'd be, like, hand-delivered to your phone."

"What are the odds? I mean, it's not *that* big a town, I guess, but still."

"We'll just say it was your mouth to God's

ear," said Everett, darting in to kiss Isabelle's cheek.

"What's her name?

"Sylvie," Everett murmured. "Her name is Sylvie." *A sweet name,* he thought.

"Well, I call this a sign," said Isabelle.

"So now what?" asked Brandon. "You can't just up and say, 'Hey, I bought your grandmother's ring and I've been trying to find you for two months to return it,'" warned Brandon. "You'd look like a creepy stalker guy."

"Whether you were originally looking to go out with her or not, Perfect Chemistry matched the two of you," Isabelle pointed out. "Put the issue of the ring aside for now and just strike up a conversation. Be yourself, and I'm sure she'll be charmed. I was when I met you."

"Hey!" said Brandon.

She pressed a smacking kiss to his lips. "You charmed me first. Still, Ev has this whole utterly adorable geek thing going on."

"Um, thanks," said Everett. "I think."

"Trust me. Women love beta heroes. Smart, sensitive, funny. You've got this."

He let out a breath. "I hope you're right."

"I'm not going," declared Sylvie. She plopped down on her bed in protest and crossed her bunny-slippered feet.

"Do you want to raid my closet? I know I never feel like I have anything to wear when I'm getting ready for a new date," said Brenna as she dug through Sylvie's closet. "I've got this red dress—"

"It has nothing to do with my clothes. I'm just not going. This whole thing was a mistake. I should never have let you talk me into it."

"You have to go," Brenna insisted. "He's going to be waiting for you at El Charro."

"So? If he never meets me in the first place, he doesn't even know who to be mad at."

"Apart from the fact that that's totally rude and uncool behavior, you could run into him around town somewhere. We're not *that* big a city. And then where will you be?"

"I'll be where I wanted to be before you dragged me into this mess."

Brenna turned, a little black dress in hand. "Come on, Syl, you *can't* stand the poor guy up on *Valentine's Day.* You agreed to this date."

"No, *you* agreed to this date for me. And wouldn't let me back out. Well, I'm backing out now. Who the hell goes for a first date on *Valentine's Day?* Nobody, that's who."

"First off, *you* were the one who talked to him in chat for *two hours* the last three nights running. All I did was give the answer you *should* have given before you could talk yourself out of it. Second, he admitted he didn't realize that Friday was Valentine's and offered to change the time and location to something else."

"Which you said no to for me," Sylvie reminded her.

"Because you'd have backed out of that, too. Look, it's *Mexican.* Who goes out for Mexican on Valentine's Day? Nobody serious. I'm telling you, this is a no pressure first date."

"There is no such thing as a no pressure first date." Not for her. Not anymore. God, would she ever be able to go out with a guy again without worrying he had ulterior motives or a criminal record?

"Sylvie..." Brenna put down the dress and perched on the bed. "You had a nice conversation with this guy. This is your chance to have a nice meal. Dinner is not a contract, it's not an engagement. It's not even a promise of a second date. It's just dinner. And if he turns out to be a dud, then at least you'll have gotten your favorite chips and dip."

"I can get that with you." She knew she sounded petulant, but that was better than the vague gnawing panic fluttering in her chest.

Brenna laid a hand over hers. "Honey, what are you afraid of?"

"Do you want the full list?" Sylvie scrubbed a hand over her face. "I'm...terrified. That this will be a disaster. That I'll make a fool of myself. That Everett seems like this sweet, funny guy and he'll turn out to be a jerk and a user. I *just* started to get back on my feet. And that was only through your help and some sacrifices I wish to God I hadn't had to make. I can't bear it if I have to go through all that again. I won't survive it financially or emotionally."

"That's a lot to put on a first date, sweetie."

"See?" Sylvie threw up her hands. "I've got some titanic trust issues, Brenna. Not just of men, but of myself. How can I trust my own judgment anymore?"

"Because you're a smart woman. Yeah, you made an error in judgment. But continuing to punish yourself for that insults your intelligence. You won't make the same mistake twice. If that means you date a guy for months before he ever even finds out where you live, that's fine. But all that is something to deal with down the line. Tonight you only have to deal with one thing: What you're going to wear to go have a pleasant evening with a potentially charming and funny guy."

"But what if—"

"No." Brenna held up a hand. "No what ifs allowed. Now you're going to get dressed in something that makes you feel good, and I'm going to drive you to El Charro."

"Don't you have a date with Adam tonight?"

"Not until much later. He had to work. So I'm going to take you to the restaurant and check him out with you. If we get a creeper vibe, we'll come home. Otherwise, you're going in. And you'll call me to come get you when you're done unless you feel comfortable with him bringing you home. Okay?"

Sylvie tried to think of a way to argue against that plan and couldn't think of a thing.

She was still thinking forty-five minutes later when Brenna whipped into a parking space with a view of the front door to El Charro and said, "Now, we wait."

Sylvie wished for a fishbowl margarita. Surely that would make this more bearable.

"Hey, isn't that him?" asked Brenna. "It looks like his picture at Perfect Chemistry."

Sylvie zeroed in on a lanky figure hurrying across the parking lot. His shoulders were hunched against the cold, and she could only see him in profile, but the brown hair, the build, were right. As he turned his head to scan the parking lot, she sank down in her seat.

"Oh yeah, that's him. And honey, you don't have a thing to worry about."

"Why do you say that?"

"Look at that sweater."

Sylvie leaned forward and squinted to make out the pattern. "Are those…reindeer?"

"With *fur* on the collar! There is not a con man or tool alive who would be caught dead in that thing. Obviously you made the right decision going totally casual instead of little black dress knockout."

"Bless his heart," Sylvie murmured, feeling a smile tug at the corners of her mouth. How could she be intimidated by a guy wearing *that?*

Brenna folded her arms on the steering wheel and grinned. "Doesn't that make you want to just snap him up and give him a what not to wear intervention?"

"I don't know…it's kind of adorable in a clueless sort of way."

"Well, don't just sit here. Get on in there and find out if his personality matches."

The ring in Everett's pocket seemed to have its own gravitational pull. He felt weighed down by it and half wondered why nobody seemed to notice him compulsively checking its presence. He wasn't sure he could be more nervous if he were legitimately proposing, which was absolutely ridiculous. It was supposed to be a quick, impulsive act of kindness, over and done with. Now here he was, on Valentine's Day of all days, waiting for a first date.

"Table for two," he told the hostess.

The woman's gaze flicked up, then down, seeming to linger on the bulge in his pocket.

Great, it is *noticeable,* Everett thought with disgust.

"Nice sweater," she said, her lips twitching.

Shit. That confirmed his suspicions. He looked like a complete ass in this sweater. But he'd given his coat away to Adrian Henning, the down-on-his-luck accountant, who'd come into the office for help that afternoon. The man had lost his job and then had the added insult of losing everything he owned in a house fire the week before. The case had taken longer than he'd anticipated to sort out, making arrangements for a new apartment and furnishings for Henning and his young family, pulling strings to land him an interview the following week, so there'd been no time to run home to change or even shave. It was either freeze or make do with the horrendous sweater his mom had surprised him with at Christmas. He still wasn't sure if the thing had been a serious gift or a joke.

Maybe I can get a table and get out of it before she gets here, he thought.

"Everett?"

At the sound of his name in that soft, southern drawl, he turned and promptly forgot about the heinous sweater.

Sylvie's sunny hair was loose, spilling over the shoulders of her red parka. Her mouth was curved in a half-smile that made the corners of her eyes crinkle. It was such a departure from the strained, upset woman he'd seen at Vandevelde's that, for a moment, he was struck dumb. He'd known in a purely academic sense that she was beautiful. But he'd been focused on her situation, not on the woman herself. She was absolutely stunning.

"Wow."

The half smile turned full wattage, and Everett realized he'd said that aloud. Whatever embarrassment he felt never actually manifested, as his synapses were, quite simply, fried.

"Have you been waiting long?" she asked.

The best he could manage was a shake of the head.

"This way please," said the hostess.

Right. There were other people here. In the restaurant. Where they were going to have a meal.

Everett held out his hand in an *after you* gesture. Sylvie moved by him and he loosed a breath. *Okay, buddy, get in the game.*

El Charro had decorated for the occasion. The mural painted walls were draped in twinkle lights, and the over-table lights were set to dim. Across the room, a quartet of mariachis played a bright, bouncy polka for a family of six.

Everett managed to get his brain in gear just in time to pull out a chair for Sylvie. The gesture seemed to fluster her. A blush crept across her cheeks as she eased into the spot and began to shimmy out of the coat. Circling around to the other side of the table, he blessed his mother for the endless drills on manners and etiquette. No matter how rattled he was, he could always fall back on that.

The arrival of their server with a basket of chips and salsa put off the awkward lull in conversation for a few moments longer. They both ordered a glass of wine.

"Can I interest you in any other appetizers?"

"Queso," they said in unison, and laughed.

"The great equalizer," said Everett as the waitress walked away.

"It's a personal weakness," she admitted.

"I can think of worse forms of kryptonite."

Sylvie's focus dipped down to the chips and salsa. She took one and said, "I have a confession."

"Oh yeah?" What would this be? That she recognized him from the jewelers? That she knew who he really was?

"I almost didn't come tonight. My roommate browbeat me into it."

"Oh." What else did you say to that kind of announcement?

She looked up, a hint of alarm on her face as it hit her that she might have insulted him. "It wasn't that I didn't want to meet you," she said in a rush. Her hand shot out to cover this. "I've really enjoyed chatting with you this week. But in the interest of full disclosure, I have to tell you my last relationship was a real doozy of a failure, and it's left me a little bit gun shy."

Her fingers were warm. Everett wanted to turn his hand to link with hers but didn't think she realized she'd moved, so he held still.

"Nothing wrong with being cautious," he said. "I've had my share of less than successful attempts." Women who'd looked at his name and seen dollar signs rather than him. "For what it's worth, I'm glad your roommate changed your mind."

Sylvie smiled at him again, and it arrowed straight to his chest. *Oh boy.*

"Here we go. Two white wines, one bowl of queso."

They both eased back as the waitress served them, and Everett regretted the loss of her touch.

"Do you know what you want to order, or do you need another few minutes?"

"I'm good," said Sylvie. "I eat here a lot."

"Me too. Go ahead."

As she ordered, his mind was on what she'd said. *In the interest of full disclosure.*

I should go ahead and tell her about the ring, he thought. *Get it out of the way.* He tugged out the box, fisted it in his hand beneath the table as he reeled off his order. By the time the server left, he'd already forgotten what he'd asked for. Because he was nervous again, Everett picked up the wine and sipped.

"So, I guess this is the part where we do all the get to know you stuff," said Sylvie.

A subject change. Should he defer the confession or go with the flow of the conversation?

"Are you from the area?" she asked.

Everett shook his head. "My family is based in Seattle. We used to come out here every winter to ski. I loved it so much, I moved here when I finished school."

She scooped up some cheese dip. "What'd you study?"

"Law."

"Oh, so you're an attorney?"

"Not most of the time."

There was that flicker of a smile again. "What sort of job do you have where you don't practice but some of the time?"

Maybe a discussion of his philanthropy could work its way back around to the ring. "I work for a non-profit here in town. New Day?"

"I've heard of it," she said with a nod.

"We help the unemployed with interviews, placement. Help get them suitable clothes and such. Set up living arrangements for those who've hit on hard times and need a leg up. Do a lot of work with families. And I whip out the law degree for some pro bono work from time to time, as the need arises, since sometimes those hard times are a direct result of some legal snarl up."

"What a wonderful job."

"I love it. It's really rewarding, finding ways to help people. Kind of addictive, in fact."

"Well, if you're going to have an addiction, one that's for the benefit of humanity seems like a pretty awesome one to have."

Everett jerked his shoulder in a shrug. "I've

done some pretty crazy things in the name of helping folks." The box in his hand felt hot. Or maybe that was his hand sweating.

Now or never, he thought. *Get it out there.*

Wow, what a guy, thought Sylvie. If she could've written up a request for a man as polar opposite from Neal as it was possible to get, she was pretty sure the answer would be Everett. How incredibly wonderful was that?

"You know, for the record, I'm really glad I changed my mind and came tonight," she said.

He smiled at her. "Hang on to that thought," he said.

What a strange thing to say.

"There's something I wanted to give you."

"Okay…"

Everett lifted his hand, laid something on the table. His expression was tense, an odd mix of some kind of anxiety and…maybe hope. Sylvie felt an answering wisp of unease unfurl and had the strangest desire not to look. Because she knew that whatever he'd put on the table was going to change something, and she'd just decided she liked where they were.

The mariachi band burst into song beside them. They both jolted, looking over into the musicians' grinning faces as they played what Sylvie imagined was some kind of Spanish love song. God, talk about awkward. Everett looked distressed by their presence, which was actually kind of cute. She'd already learned he was too polite to ask them to leave, so they'd both endure this uncomfortable interlude until the song was finished.

Sylvie dropped her gaze to the box on the table and her mind went utterly blank as she stared at it.

A ring box.

He'd brought her a ring.

On Valentine's Day.

Oh God.

Panic and mortification burst to life inside her. Of course, he wasn't as amazing as he seemed. He was crazy. He was *proposing* on their *first date?* They didn't even know each other's *last names!*

Sylvie pushed back from the table, fumbling to grab for her coat and purse. Everett was trying to say something, but she couldn't hear anything over the music and the roaring in her ears. "I'm sorry. I'm sorry, but I have to go."

Everybody was *staring*. She had to get the hell out of here. Skirting around another table, she managed to get past the band and made a beeline for the exit, not quite running. Everett got caught by the musicians. She could hear him uttering apologies as he tried to get past them. Dear God, were they *following him?* She was already to the hostess station when he called her name.

"Sylvie, wait!"

She didn't, instead shoving her arms into the coat and heading for the door, weaving through the patrons waiting for tables.

"It's not what you think!"

Sylvie hit the door, burst out into the cold

night. What was she going to do? Brenna had driven her. It would take a good fifteen minutes for her to get here.

I should've hidden in the restroom, she thought. It was too late now. The door behind her was already opening.

"Sylvie, please just listen."

She glanced over her shoulder. Amazing how he didn't look or sound like a crazy person. But maybe that was the thing. Maybe crazy didn't show on the outside. "Everett, I'm sorry, but I really can't do this. I apologize if I've given you the impression—" *Of what? That I was also a lunatic?* "—that I'm looking for something serious, but I—"

"Sylvie, it's your grandmother's ring."

Whatever response she'd expected from him, it wasn't that. "What?"

"Just listen, please."

She turned toward him fully, then, holding her purse by the strap in case she needed to hit him with it. "I'm listening."

"This is not a proposal. I'm not a lunatic, I

swear."

"That's what a lunatic would say, I expect."

He tipped his head and laughed a little. "Fair point. Look, I was there, at Vandevelde's the day you sold your grandmother's ring."

"You what?" She wracked her brain, but she could remember only the jeweler himself. Then again, she'd been so distraught, a T-Rex could've walked by outside, and she'd probably have missed it.

"I came into the store with a friend of mine who was there to buy an engagement ring. I overheard part of what you told Mr. Vandevelde about why you were selling. I told you, I've done some crazy stuff in the name of helping people. This might be one of the craziest. Right after you walked out, I bought the ring because I wanted to give it back to you. But by the time I made it out of the store, I'd lost you. So I've been carrying it around for the last two months, hoping to run into you again. When I ran across you on Perfect Chemistry, I thought, finally, I'd get the chance to return this to its rightful owner." He held out the now open box.

She could see her grandmother's familiar sapphire ring nestled in the velvet.

"Please, take it," said Everett.

She wanted to. Oh, how she wanted to. But what would he expect in return? "What do you get out of this?" she asked instead.

"The satisfaction of knowing an heirloom went back to the family it came from."

"You're trying to convince me that you're not nuts, but you're failing miserably. Everett, people don't go around spending thousands on a whim to give something back to a complete stranger. Not with no strings attached. Nobody is that selfless."

"You should talk to my friend Brandon. He's always on me about doing stuff like this. Figures I did enough when I started New Day. But what the hell good is an inheritance if you can't spend it to make people's lives better?"

Sylvie stared at him. He'd *started* New Day? It was *his* company? She'd thought he was Neal's opposite, but she had no way of knowing how right she'd been. Neal had been a selfish con man, pretending to be rich to take advantage of the unsuspecting. And here was Everett, apparently legitimately wealthy, trying to use that wealth for the benefit of others.

When Everett took a step to close the distance between them, Sylvie held her ground.

"You don't owe me a date or dinner or even a chance to ever see you again, if you don't want." He lifted her hand, curled her fingers around the box. "This belongs to you." He stepped away and put his hands behind his back, as if to keep her from handing the ring over again. "It's paid for, free and clear. You can check with Mr. Vandevelde yourself, if you want."

"I believe you," she murmured. The stones glittered in the faint wash of light from El Charro. Sylvie ran a light finger over them, feeling the comforting contours. Her grandmother's ring, back in her hand. Because of the extraordinary kindness of a stranger. Throat tight with emotion, she looked up at Everett. "Can you possibly be for real?"

He reached over and pinched his wrist. "Ow. See, flesh and blood. Seriously, my only motive was to do something spontaneous and nice for someone at Christmas. I didn't—don't expect anything in return. You don't have to finish dinner, even. If you want to go on home, I absolutely understand."

He meant it. Sylvie could see it in his face.

What a guy, she thought again.

Saying nothing, she reached up and unclasped the chain around her neck, sliding the ring back on. Feeling the faint weight of it settle against her chest, something inside her eased and opened. With a sigh, she stepped toward Everett and laid a hand against his cheek. "You can't know what this means to me."

But Everett did know. He could see it in her eyes, feel it in the careful way she cupped his cheek. And he was pretty sure that no matter how many people he helped, in how many ways, nothing else was ever going to feel quite like this, mean quite this much to him personally.

"Glad I could help," he said, his voice a trifle ragged at the edges.

"Thank you," said Sylvie. She eased in closer, rose to her toes.

Everett froze. "You don't have to—"

"I know," she said and laid her lips over his.

Just a light, sweet pressure, but his heart leapt into his throat. His hands fisted to keep from reaching for her, and it took everything he had to hold himself still, accepting what she offered without giving any pressure in return. Her body swayed closer, the warmth of her thighs, belly, chest brushing up against his, cooking what remained of his brain cells, making him want to touch. Everett fought back a groan. He was pretty sure this might kill him, but he'd be damned if he'd do anything to make her feel threatened or used.

Sylvie eased back, just a fraction, hand still curved against his cheek.

Everett swallowed hard, eyes still closed. "You're welcome," he managed.

"Everett?" she said softly.

"Yeah?" He should really open his eyes now, but he didn't want to lose the remembered sensation of her mouth on his.

"You could kiss me back. I wouldn't mind."

His eyes popped open at that to find her mouth curved in that half smile again. God, if she had any idea what that smile did to him.

Sylvie's hand slid from his face to twine in the hair at his nape. Everett framed her face, loving the smooth feel of her skin against his palms as he lowered his lips to hers, tasted her smile. She sighed and softened against him, a surrender that had him angling his head, diving just a little bit deeper to torture them both. Her arms wrapped around him, but he kept his hands at her face, where they were safe and in control. He stroked the edge of her cheekbones with his thumbs and enjoyed one last taste before edging back.

"Wow," he said again.

"I own an art gallery," blurted Sylvie.

Everett blinked at her. "Sorry?"

"I've been letting you do all the talking. Before this little diversion, we were working on that get to know each other portion of the night. I figured maybe it was time for some quid pro quo." Her smiled turned suddenly shy. "That is, if you'd still like to see me."

Everett smiled and dropped his brow to hers. "I would. I really really would."

"Do you suppose they've already cleared our table?"

"If they have, we can start over," he said. "No agenda, no weirdness."

"I'd like that," she said.

Tucking Sylvie's hand in his, Everett opened the door to El Charro and led them both to a new beginning.

Copyright 2014 Kait Nolan

A complete and up-to-date list of all my books can be found at https://kaitnolan.com.

THE MISFIT INN SERIES
SMALL TOWN FAMILY ROMANCE

- *When You Got A Good Thing* (Kennedy and Xander)
- *Til There Was You* (Misty and Denver)

- *Those Sweet Words* (Pru and Flynn)
- *Stay A Little Longer* (Athena and Logan)
- *Bring It On Home* (Maggie and Porter)

RESCUE MY HEART SERIES
SMALL TOWN MILITARY ROMANCE

- *Baby It's Cold Outside* (Ivy and Harrison)
- *What I Like About You* (Laurel and Sebastian)
- *Bad Case of Loving You* (Paisley and Ty prequel)
- *Made For Loving You* (Paisley and Ty)

MEN OF THE MISFIT INN
SMALL TOWN SOUTHERN ROMANCE

- *Let It Be Me* (Emerson and Caleb)
- *Our Kind of Love* (Abbey and Kyle)

WISHFUL SERIES

SMALL TOWN SOUTHERN ROMANCE

- *Once Upon A Coffee* (Avery and Dillon)
- *To Get Me To You* (Cam and Norah)
- *Know Me Well* (Liam and Riley)
- *Be Careful, It's My Heart* (Brody and Tyler)
- *Just For This Moment* (Myles and Piper)
- *Wish I Might* (Reed and Cecily)
- *Turn My World Around* (Tucker and Corinne)
- *Dance Me A Dream* (Jace and Tara)
- *See You Again* (Trey and Sandy)
- *The Christmas Fountain* (Chad and Mary Alice)
- *You Were Meant For Me* (Mitch and Tess)
- *A Lot Like Christmas* (Ryan and Hannah)
- *Dancing Away With My Heart* (Zach and Lexi)

WISHING FOR A HERO SERIES (A WISHFUL SPINOFF SERIES)
SMALL TOWN ROMANTIC SUSPENSE

- *Make You Feel My Love* (Judd and Autumn)
- *Watch Over Me* (Nash and Rowan)
- *Can't Take My Eyes Off You* (Ethan and Miranda)
- *Burn For You* (Sean and Delaney)

MEET CUTE ROMANCE
SMALL TOWN SHORT ROMANCE

- *Once Upon A Snow Day*
- *Once Upon A New Year's Eve*
- *Once Upon An Heirloom*
- *Once Upon A Coffee*
- *Once Upon A Campfire*
- *Once Upon A Rescue*

SUMMER CAMP
CONTEMPORARY ROMANCE

- *Once Upon A Campfire*
- *Second Chance Summer*

Kait is a Mississippi native, who often swears like a sailor, calls everyone sugar, honey, or darlin', and can wield a bless your heart like a saber or a Snuggie, depending on requirements.

You can find more information on this

RITA ® Award-winning author and her books on her website http://kaitnolan.com. While you're there, sign up for her newsletter so you don't miss out on news about new releases!